D1532057

DATE DUE

messenger

LOIS LOWRY

messenger

LAUREL-LEAF BOOKS

Published by Laurel-Leaf
an imprint of
Random House Children's Books
a division of Random House, Inc.
New York

This is a work of fiction. Names, characters, places, and
incidents either are the product of the author's imagination
or are used fictitiously. Any resemblance to actual persons,
living or dead, events, or locales is entirely coincidental.

Originally published in hardcover in the United States by
Houghton Mifflin Company, New York, in 2004. This edition
published by arrangement with Houghton Mifflin Company.

Laurel-Leaf and colophon are registered
trademarks of Random House, Inc.

www.randomhouse.com/teens

Educators and librarians, for a variety of teaching tools,
visit us at www.randomhouse.com/teachers

ISBN: 0-440-23912-5

January 2006

Printed in the United States of America

18 17 16 15 14 13

1

Matty was impatient to have the supper preparations over and done with. He wanted to cook, eat, and be gone. He wished he were grown so that he could decide when to eat, or whether to bother eating at all. There was something he needed to do, a thing that scared him. Waiting just made it worse.

Matty was no longer a boy, but not yet a man. Sometimes, standing outside the homeplace, he measured himself against the window. Once he had stood only to its sill, his forehead there, pressing into the wood, but now he was so tall he could see inside without effort. Or, moving back in the high grass, he could see himself reflected in the glass pane. His face was becoming manly, he thought, though childishly he still enjoyed making scowls and frowns at his own reflection. His voice was deepening.

He lived with the blind man, the one they called Seer, and helped him. He cleaned the homeplace, though cleaning bored him. The man said it was necessary. So Matty swept the wooden floor each day and straightened the bedcovers: neatly on the man's bed, with haphazard indifference on his own, in the room next to the kitchen. They shared the cooking. The man laughed at Matty's concoctions and tried to teach him, but Matty was impatient and didn't care about the subtlety of herbs.

"We can just put it all together in the pot," Matty insisted. "It all goes together in our bellies anyway."

It was a long-standing and friendly argument. Seer chuckled. "Smell this," he said, and held out the pale green shoot that he'd been chopping.

Matty sniffed dutifully. "Onion," he said, and shrugged. "We can just throw it in.

"Or," he added, "we don't even need to cook it. But then our breath stinks. There's a girl promised she'd kiss me if I have sweet breath. But I think she's teasing."

The blind man smiled in the boy's direction. "Teasing's part of the fun that comes before kissing," he told Matty, whose face had flushed pink with embarrassment.

"You could trade for a kiss," the blind man suggested with a chuckle. "What would you give? Your fishing pole?"

"Don't. Don't joke about the trading."

"You're right, I shouldn't. It used to be a light-hearted thing. But now—you're right, Matty. It's not to be laughed at anymore."

"My friend Ramon went to the last Trade Mart, with his parents. But he won't talk about it."

"We won't then, either. Is the butter melted in the pan?"

Matty looked. The butter was bubbling slightly and golden brown. "Yes."

"Add the onion, then. Stir it so it doesn't burn."

Matty obeyed.

"Now smell *that*," the blind man said. Matty sniffed. The gently sautéing onion released an aroma that made his mouth water.

"Better than raw?" Seer asked.

"But a bother," Matty replied impatiently. "Cooking's a bother."

"Add some sugar. Just a pinch or two. Let it cook for a minute and then we'll put the rabbit in. Don't be so impatient, Matty. You always want to rush things, and there's no need."

"I want to go out before night comes. I have something to check. I need to eat supper and get out there to the clearing before it's dark."

The blind man laughed. He picked up the rabbit parts from the table, and as always, Matty was amazed at how sure his hands were, how he knew just where things had been left. He watched while the man deftly patted flour onto the pieces of meat and then added the rabbit to the pan. The aroma changed when the meat sizzled next to the softened onion. The man added a handful of herbs.

"It doesn't matter to *you* if it's dark or light outside," Matty told him, scowling, "but I need the daylight to look at something."

"What something is that?" Seer asked, then added, "When the meat has browned, add some broth so it doesn't stick to the pan."

Matty obeyed, tilting into the pan the bowl of broth in which the rabbit had been boiled earlier. The dark liquid picked up chunks of onion and chopped herbs, and swirled them around the pieces of meat. He knew to put the lid on now, and to turn the fire low. The stew simmered and he began to set the plates on the table where they would have their supper together.

He hoped the blind man would forget that he had asked *what something*. He didn't want to tell. Matty was puzzled by what he had hidden in the clearing. It frightened him, not knowing what it meant. He wondered for a moment whether he could trade it away.

∽

When, finally, the supper dishes were washed and put away, and the blind man sat in the cushioned chair and picked up the stringed instrument that he played in the evening, Matty inched his way to the door, hoping to slip away unnoticed. But the man heard everything that moved. Matty had known him to hear a spider scurry from one side of its web to another.

"Off to Forest again?"

Matty sighed. No escaping. "I'll be back by dark."

4

"Could be. But light the lamp, in case you're late. After dark it's nice to have window light to aim for. I remember what Forest was like at night."

"Remember from when?"

The man smiled. "From when I could see. Long before you were born."

"Were you scared of Forest?" Matty asked him. So many people were, and with good reason.

"No. It's all an illusion."

Matty frowned. He didn't know what the blind man meant. Was he saying that fear was an illusion? Or that Forest was? He glanced over. The blind man was rubbing the polished wooden side of his instrument with a soft cloth. His thoughts had turned to the smooth wood, though he couldn't see the golden maple with its curly grain. Maybe, Matty thought, *everything* was an illusion to a man who had lost his eyes.

Matty lengthened the wick and checked the lamp to be certain there was oil. Then he struck a match.

"Now you're glad I made you clean the soot from the lamp chimneys, aren't you?" The blind man didn't expect an answer. He moved his fingers on the strings, listening for the tone. Carefully, as he did most evenings, he tuned the instrument. He could hear variations in sounds that seemed to the boy to be all the same. Matty stood in the doorway for a moment, watching. On the table, the lamp flickered. The man sat with his head tilted toward the window so that the summer early-evening light outlined the scars on his face. He listened, then turned a small screw on the back of the instrument's wooden neck, then listened again. Now he was concentrating on the sounds, and had forgotten the boy. Matty slipped away.

∿

Heading for the path that entered Forest at the edge of Village, Matty went by a roundabout way so that he could pass the home of the schoolteacher, a good-hearted man with a deep red stain that covered half of his face. Birthmark, it was called. When Matty was new to Village, he had sometimes found himself staring at the man because he had never known anyone before with such a mark. Where Matty had come from, flaws like that were not allowed. People were put to death for less.

But here in Village, marks and failings were not considered flaws at all. They were valued. The blind man had been given the true name Seer and was respected for the special vision that he had behind his ruined eyes.

The schoolteacher, though his true name was Mentor, was sometimes affectionately called "Rosy" by the children because of the crimson birthmark that spread across his face. Children loved him. He was a wise and patient teacher. Matty, just a boy when he first came here to live with the blind man, had attended school full time for a while, and still went for added learning on winter afternoons. Mentor had been the one who taught him to sit still, to listen, and eventually to read.

He passed by the schoolteacher's house not to see Mentor, or to admire the lavish flower garden, but in hopes of seeing the schoolteacher's pretty daughter, who was named Jean and who had recently teased Matty with the promise of a kiss. Often she was in the garden, weeding, in the evenings.

But tonight there was no sign of her, or her father. Matty saw a fat spotted dog sleeping on the porch, but it appeared that no one was at home.

Just as well, he thought. Jean would have delayed him with her giggles and teasing promises—which always came to nothing, and Matty knew that she made them to all the boys—and he should not even have made the side trip in hopes of seeing her.

He took a stick and drew a heart in the dirt on the path beside her garden. Carefully he put her name in the heart, and his own below it. Maybe she would see it and know he had been there, and maybe she would care.

"Hey, Matty! What are you doing?" It was his friend Ramon, coming around the corner. "Have you had supper? Want to come eat with us?"

Quickly Matty moved toward Ramon, hiding the heart traced in the dirt behind him and hoping his friend wouldn't notice it. It was always fun, in a way, to go to Ramon's homeplace, because his family had recently traded for something called a Gaming

Machine, a large decorated box with a handle that you pulled to make three wheels spin around inside. Then a bell rang and the wheels stopped at a small window. If their pictures matched, the machine spit out a chunk of candy. It was very exciting to play.

Sometimes he wondered what they had sacrificed for the Gaming Machine, but one never asked.

"We ate already," he said. "I have to go someplace before it gets dark, so we ate early."

"I'd come with you, but I have a cough, and Herbalist said I shouldn't run around too much. I promised to go right home," Ramon said. "But if you wait, I'll run and ask . . ."

"No," Matty replied quickly. "I have to go alone."

"Oh, it's for a message?"

It wasn't, but Matty nodded. It bothered him a little to lie about small things. But he always had; he had grown up lying, and he still found it strange that the people in this place where he now lived thought lying was wrong. To Matty, it was sometimes a way of making things easier, more comfortable, more convenient.

"See you tomorrow, then." Ramon waved and hurried on toward his own homeplace.

❧

Matty knew the paths of Forest as if he had made them. And indeed, some of them *were* of his making, over the years. The roots had flattened as he made his way here and there, seeking the shortest, safest route from place to place. He was swift and quiet in the woods, and he could feel the direction of things without landmarks, in the same way that he could feel weather and was able to predict rain long before the clouds came or there was a shift in wind. Matty simply *knew*.

Others from Village rarely ventured into Forest. It was dangerous for them. Sometimes Forest closed in and entangled people who had tried to travel beyond. There had been terrible deaths, with bodies brought out strangled by vines or branches that had reached out malevolently around the throats and limbs of those who decided to leave Village. Somehow Forest knew. Somehow, too, it knew that Matty's travels were benign and necessary. The vines had never reached out for him. The trees seemed, sometimes, almost to part and usher him through.

"Forest likes me," he had proudly commented once to the blind man.

Seer had agreed. "Maybe it needs you," he pointed out.

The people needed Matty, too. They trusted him to know the paths, to be safe on them, and to do the errands that required traveling through the thick woods with its complicated, mazelike turnings. He carried messages for them. It was his job. He thought that when it came time to be assigned his true name, *Messenger* would be the choice. He liked the sound of it and looked forward to taking that title.

But this evening Matty was not carrying or collecting a message, though he had fibbed and told Ramon so. He headed to a clearing he knew of, a place that lay just beyond a thick stand of bristly pines. Deftly he jumped a small brook, then turned off the worn path to proceed between two trees, pushing his way through. These trees had grown fast in recent years, and now the clearing was completely concealed and had become Matty's private place.

He needed privacy for this thing he was discovering about himself: a place to test it in secret, to weigh his own fear for what it meant.

It was dim in the clearing. Behind him, the sun was starting to set over Village, and the light that reached down through Forest was pinkish and pale. Matty made his way across the mossy ground of the clearing to a thicket of tall ferns near the base of a tree. He squatted there and listened, leaning his head toward the ferns. Softly he made a sound, one he had practiced; a brief moment later, he heard the sound he had both hoped and dreaded to hear, in response.

He reached gently into the undergrowth and lifted out a small frog. From his hand, it looked up at him through bulging, unafraid eyes, and made the sound again: *churrump*.

Churrump.

Churrump.

Matty repeated the frog's throaty sound, as if they were conversing. Though he was nervous, the back-and-forth sounds made him laugh a little. He examined the slick green body carefully. The frog made no effort to leap from his hand. It was passive in his palm, and the deep translucent throat quivered.

He found what he was looking for. In a way, he had hoped he would not. His life would be easier, Matty knew, if the little frog were unmarked and ordinary. But it was not; he had known it would not be; and he knew that things were all shifting for him now. His future had taken a new and secret turn. It was not the frog's fault, he realized, and gently he replaced the small green creature in the tall ferns and watched the fronds tremble as it moved away, unaware. He realized that he was trembling as well.

∾

Returning to Village along the path that was deep in shadows now, Matty heard sounds from the area beyond the marketplace. At first he thought in surprise that people were singing. Singing was common in Village, but usually not outdoors, not in the evening. Puzzled, he paused and listened. It was not singing at all, Matty realized, but the rhythmic and mournful sound they called keening, the sound of loss. He set aside his other worries and began to hurry through the evening's last light to the homeplace, where the blind man would be waiting and would explain.

11

2

"Did you hear about what happened to Gatherer last night? He tried to go back but it had been too long." Ramon and Matty, carrying their fishing rods, had met for an excursion to catch salmon, and Ramon was bursting with the news.

Matty winced at what his friend said. So Gatherer had been taken by Forest. He was a cheerful man who loved children and small animals, who smiled often and told boisterous jokes.

Ramon spoke in the self-important tone of one who likes being a conveyor of news. Matty was very fond of his friend but sometimes suspected that his true name might eventually turn out to be Boaster.

"How do you know?"

"They found him last night on the path behind the schoolhouse. After I left you, I heard the commotion. I saw them bring his body in."

"I heard the noise. Seer and I thought it must be someone taken."

Matty had arrived at the homeplace the night before to find the blind man preparing for bed and listening attentively to the low collective moan, clearly a large number of people grieving.

"Someone's been lost," the blind man had said with a worried look, pausing while unbuckling his shoes. He sat on his bed, dressed in his nightshirt.

"Should I take a message to Leader?"

"He'll know already, from the sound. It's a keening."

"Should we go?" Matty asked him. In a way, he had wanted to. He had never attended a keening. But in another way, he was relieved to see the blind man shake his head no.

"They have enough. It sounds like a good-sized group; I can hear at least twelve."

As always, Matty was amazed at the capacity of the blind man's perceptions. He himself heard only the chorus of wails. "Twelve?" he asked, and then teased, "Are you sure it's not eleven, or thirteen?"

"I hear at least seven women," the blind man said, not noticing that Matty had intended it as a joke. "Each has a different pitch. And I think five men, though one is quite young, maybe your age. The voice is not as deep as it will be later. It may be that friend of yours; what's his name?"

"Ramon?"

"Yes. I think I hear Ramon's voice. He's hoarse."

"Yes, he has a cough. He's taking herbs for it."

Now, recalling it, Matty asked his friend, "Did you keen? I think we may have heard you."

"Yes. They had enough. But since I was there, they let me join. I have this cough, though, so my voice wasn't very good. I only went because I wanted to see the body. I've never seen one."

"Of course you have. You were with me when we watched them lay out Stocktender for burial. And you saw that little girl after she fell in the river and they pulled her out drowned. I remember you were there."

"I meant entangled," Ramon explained. "I've seen plenty of dead. But till last night I never saw one entangled."

Neither had Matty. He had only heard of it. Entangling happened so rarely that he had begun to think of it as a myth, something from the past. "What was it like? They say it's hideous."

Ramon nodded. "It was. It looked as if first the vines grabbed him by the neck and pulled tight. Poor Gatherer. He had grabbed at them to pull loose but then they curled around his hands as well. He was completely entangled. The look on his face was fearsome. His eyes were open but twigs and all had started to enter under the lids. And they were in his mouth, too. I could see something wrapped around his tongue."

Matty shuddered. "He was such a nice man," he said. "He always tossed berries to us when he was out gathering. I would open my mouth wide and he would aim for it. If I caught a berry in my mouth he cheered and gave me extra."

"Me too." Ramon looked sad. "And his wife has a new baby. Someone said that's why he went. He wanted to go tell her family about the baby."

"But didn't he know what would happen? Hadn't he received Warnings?"

Ramon coughed suddenly. He bent over and gasped. Then he straightened up and shrugged. "His wife says not. He went once before, when their first child was born, and had no trouble. No Warning."

Matty thought about it. Gatherer must have overlooked a Warning. The early ones were sometimes small. He felt great sadness for the gentle, happy man who had been so brutally entangled and had left two children fatherless. Forest always gave Warnings, Matty knew. He entered so often himself and always was watchful. If he had one Warning, even the smallest, he would never enter again. The blind man had entered only once, to return to his original village when it needed his wisdom. He had come back safely, but he had had a small Warning on his return: a sudden painful puncture from what had seemed a tiny twig. He couldn't see it, of course, though later he said he had felt it come forward, had perceived it with the kind of knowledge that had made the people designate Seer as his true name. But Matty, still a young boy, had been with him then, as a guide; and Matty had seen the twig grow, expand, sharpen, aim itself, and stab. There was no question. It was a Warning. The blind man could never enter Forest again. His time for going back had ended.

Yet Matty had never been warned. Again and again he entered Forest, moved along its trails, spoke to its creatures. He understood that for some reason, he was special to Forest. He had traveled its paths for years, six years now, since that first time, when he was still very young and had left the home that had been cruel to him.

"I'm never going in," Ramon said firmly. "Not after seeing what it did to Gatherer."

"You don't have a place to go back to," Matty pointed out. "You were born in Village. It's only those who try to go back to someplace that they left once."

"Like you, maybe."

"Like me, except I'm careful."

"I'm not taking the chance. Is this a good place to fish?" Ramon asked, changing the subject. "I don't want to walk any farther. I'm tired all the time lately." They had been ambling toward the river, skirting the cornfield, and had reached the grassy bank where they often fished together. "We caught a lot here last time. My mother cooked some for dinner, but there were so many that I nibbled on leftovers while I was playing the Gaming Machine after dinner."

The Gaming Machine again. Ramon mentioned it so often. Maybe *Gloater* would be his true name, Matty thought. He had already decided on Boaster, but now, in his mind, he decided Gloater was more appropriate. Or Bragger. He was tired of hearing about the Gaming Machine. And a little jealous, too.

"Yes, here," Matty said. He scrambled down the

slippery bank to the place where a boulder, large enough to stand on, jutted out. Both boys climbed the huge outcropping of rock and settled at the top to prepare their fishing gear and cast their lines for salmon.

Behind them, Village, quiet and peaceful, continued its daily life. Gatherer had been buried this morning. With her toddler playing on the floor by her feet, his widow now nursed her new baby on the porch of her homeplace, attended by comforting women who sat with their knitting and embroidery and spoke only of happy things.

In the schoolhouse, Mentor, the schoolteacher, gently tutored a mischievous eight-year-old named Gabe, who had neglected his studies to play and now needed help. His daughter, Jean, sold flower bouquets and loaves of fresh-baked bread in her marketplace stall while she flirted, laughing, with the gangly, self-conscious boys who stopped by.

The blind man, Seer, made his way through the lanes of Village, checking on the populace, assessing the well-being of each individual. He knew each fence post, each crossroad, each voice and smell and shadow. If anything was amiss, he would do his best to make it right.

From a window, the tall young man known as Leader looked down and watched the slow and cheerful pace of Village, of the people he loved, who had chosen him to rule and guard them. He had come here as a boy, finding his way with great difficulty. The Museum held the remains of a broken sled in a glass case, and the inscription explained that it had been Leader's arrival vehicle. There were many relics of arrival in the Museum, because each person who had not been born in Village had his own story of coming there. The blind man's history was told there, too: how he had been carried, near dead, from the place where enemies had left him with his eyes torn out and his future in his own place gone.

In the Museum's glass cases there were shoes and canes and bicycles and a wheeled chair. But somehow the small red-painted sled had become a symbol of courage and hope. Leader was young but he represented those things. He had never tried to go back, never wanted to. This was his home now, these his people. As he did every afternoon, he stood at the window and watched. His eyes were a pale, piercing blue.

He watched with gratitude as the blind man moved through the lanes.

He could see beyond a porch railing to the young woman who rocked an infant and mourned her husband. *Grieve gently,* he thought.

He could see beyond the cornfield to where two young boys named Matty and Ramon were dangling lines into the river. *Good fishing,* he thought.

He could see beyond the marketplace to the cemetery where Gatherer's ruined body had been buried. *Rest in peace,* he thought.

Finally he looked toward the border of Village, to

the place where the path entered Forest and became shrouded in shadows. Leader could see beyond the shadows but was not certain what he saw. It was blurred, but there was something in Forest that disturbed Leader's consciousness and made him uneasy. He could not tell whether it was good or bad. Not yet.

∾

Deep in the thick undergrowth near the clearing, at the edge of Leader's puzzled awareness, a small green frog ate an insect it had caught with its sticky, fast-darting tongue. Squatting, it moved its protruding eyes around, trying to sense more insects to devour. Finding nothing, it hopped away. One back leg was oddly stiff but the frog barely noticed.

3

"If we had a Gaming Machine," Matty commented in a studied, offhand manner, "our evenings would never be boring."

"You think our evenings are boring, Matty? I thought you enjoyed our reading together."

Seer laughed, and corrected himself. "Sorry. I meant your reading to me, Matty, and my listening. It's my favorite time of day."

Matty shrugged. "No, I like reading to you, Seer. But I meant it's not *exciting*."

"Well, we should choose a different book, perhaps. That last one—I've forgotten its name, Matty—was a little slow-going. *Moby Dick*. That was the one."

"It was okay," Matty conceded. "But it was too long."

"Well, ask at the library for something that would move along more quickly."

"Did I explain to you how a Gaming Machine works, Seer? It moves very quickly."

The blind man chuckled. He had heard it all before, many times. "Run out to the garden and get a head of lettuce, Matty, while I finish cleaning the fish. Then you can make a salad while the fish cooks."

"And *also*," Matty continued in a loud voice as he headed for the garden just beyond the door, "it would be a nice end to a meal. Something sweet. Sort of a dessert. I did tell you, didn't I, how the Gaming Machine gives you a candy when you win?"

"See if there's a nice ripe tomato while you're out there getting the lettuce. A *sweet* one," Seer suggested in an amused voice.

"You might get a peppermint," Matty went on, "or a gumdrop, or maybe something they call a sour-ball." Beside the back step he reached into the vegetable garden and uprooted a small head of lettuce. As an afterthought, he pinched a cucumber loose from its vine nearby, and pulled some leaves from a clump of basil. Back in the kitchen, he put the salad things in the sink and halfheartedly began to wash them.

"Sourballs come in different colors, and each color is a flavor," he announced, "but I suppose that wouldn't interest you."

Matty sighed. He looked around. Even though he knew the blind man wouldn't see his gesture, he pointed to the nearby wall, which was decorated by a colorful wall-hanging, a gift from the blind man's talented daughter. Matty stood often before it, look-ing carefully at the intricate embroidered tapestry depicting a large thick forest separating two small villages far from each other. It was the geography of his own life, and that of the blind man, for they had both moved from that place to this other, with great difficulty.

"The Gaming Machine could stand right there," he decided. "It would be very convenient. *Extremely* convenient," he added, aware that the blind man liked it when he exercised his vocabulary.

Seer went to the sink, moved the washed lettuce to the side, and began to rinse the cleaned salmon steaks. "And so we would give up—or maybe even trade away—reading, and music, in exchange for the *extreme* excitement of pulling a handle and watching sourballs spit forth from a mechanical device?" he asked.

Put that way, Matty thought, the Gaming Machine didn't actually seem such a good trade. "Well," he said, "it's fun."

"Fun," the blind man repeated. "Is the stove ready? And the pan?"

Matty looked at the stove. "In a minute," he said. He stirred the burning wood a bit so that the fire flared. Then he placed the oiled pan on top. "I'll do the fish," he said, "if you fix the salad.

"I brought some basil in, too," he added, with a grin, "just because you're such a salad perfectionist. It's right there beside the lettuce." He watched while the blind man's deft hands found the basil and tore the leaves into the wooden bowl.

Then Matty took the fish and laid it in the pan, swirling the oil around. In a moment the aroma of the sautéing salmon filled the room.

Outside, it was twilight. Matty adjusted the wick on an oil lamp and lighted it. "You know," he remarked, "when you win a candy, a bell rings and colored lights blink. Of course that wouldn't matter to *you*," he added, "but some of us would really appreciate—"

"Matty, Matty, Matty," the blind man said. "Keep an eye on that fish. It cooks quickly. No bell rings when it's done.

"And don't forget," he added, "that they traded for that Gaming Machine. It probably came at a high cost."

Matty frowned. "Sometimes you get licorice," he said as a last attempt.

"Do you know what they traded? Has Ramon told you?"

"No. Nobody ever tells."

"Maybe he doesn't even know. Maybe his parents didn't tell him. That's probably good."

Matty took the pan from the stove and slid the browned fish onto two plates, one after the other. He placed them on the table and brought the salad bowl from the sink. "It's ready," he said.

The blind man went to the bread container and found two thick pieces of bread that smelled fresh-baked. "I got this at the marketplace this morning," he said, "from Mentor's daughter. She'll make someone a good wife. Is she as pretty as her voice makes her sound?"

But Matty was not going to be diverted by reminders of the schoolteacher's pretty daughter. "When's the next Trade Mart?" he asked, when they were both seated.

"You're too young."

"I heard that there was one coming soon."

"Pay no attention to what you hear. You're too young."

"I won't be always. I ought to watch."

The blind man shook his head. "It would be painful," he said. "Eat your fish now, Matty, while it's warm."

Matty poked at the salmon with his fork. He could tell that there was to be no more discussion of trading. The blind man had never traded, not one single time, and was proud of it. But Matty thought that someday he himself would. Maybe not for a Gaming Machine. But there were other things that Matty wanted. He ought to be allowed to know how the trading worked.

He decided he would find out. But first he had the other thing to worry about, and the troubling awareness that he had not dared to tell the blind man of it.

❧

There were no secrets in Village. It was one of the rules that Leader had proposed, and all of the people had voted in favor of it. Everyone who had come to Village from elsewhere, all of those who had not been

24

born here, had come from places with secrets. Sometimes—not very often, for inevitably it caused sadness—people described their places of origin: places with cruel governments, harsh punishments, desperate poverty, or false comforts.

There were so many such places. Sometimes, hearing the stories, remembering his own childhood, Matty was astounded. At first, having found his way to Village, he had thought his own brutal beginnings—a fatherless hovel for a home; a grim, defeated mother who beat him and his brother bloody—were unusual. But now he knew that there were communities everywhere, sprinkled across the vast landscape of the known world, in which people suffered. Not always from beatings and hunger, the way he had. But from ignorance. From *not knowing*. From being kept from knowledge.

He believed in Leader, and in Leader's insistence that all of Village's citizens, even the children, read, learn, participate, and care for one another. So Matty studied and did his best.

But sometimes he slipped back into the habits of his earlier life, when he had been a sly and deceitful boy in order to survive.

"I can't help it," he had argued glumly to the blind man, in the beginning of their life together, when he had been caught in some small transgression. "It's what I learnt."

"*Learned.*" The correction was gentle.

"Learned," Matty had repeated.

"Now you are relearning. You are learning honesty. I'm sorry to punish you, Matty, but Village is a population of honest and decent people, and I want you to be one of us."

Matty had hung his head. "So you'll beat me?"

"No, your punishment will be no lessons today. You will help me in the garden instead of going to school."

It had seemed, to Matty then, a laughable punishment. Who wanted to go to school, anyway? Not him!

Yet, when he was deprived of it, and could hear the other children reciting and singing in the schoolhouse, he felt woefully lost. Gradually he had learned to change his behavior and to become one of Village's happy children, and soon a good student. Now half grown and soon to finish school, he slipped only occasionally into old bad habits and almost always caught himself when he did.

It bothered Matty greatly, now, having a secret.

4

Leader had summoned Matty for message-running.

Matty enjoyed going to Leader's homeplace, because of the stairs—others had stairs, though Matty and the blind man did not, but Leader's stairs were circular, which fascinated Matty, and he liked going up and down—and because of the books. Others had books, too. Matty had a few school-books, and he often borrowed other books from the library so that he could read stories to the blind man in the evenings, a time they both enjoyed.

But Leader's homeplace, where he lived alone, had more books than Matty had ever seen in one place. The entire ground floor, except for the kitchen to one side, was lined with shelves, and the shelves were filled with volumes of every sort. Leader allowed Matty to lift down and look at any one he wanted. There were stories, of course, not unlike the ones he found in the library. There were history books as well, like those he studied at school, the best ones filled with maps that showed how the world had changed over centuries. Some books had shiny pages

27

that showed paintings of landscapes unlike anything Matty had ever seen, or of people costumed in odd ways, or of battles, and there were many quiet painted scenes of a woman holding a newborn child. Still others were written in languages from the past and from other places.

Leader laughed wryly when Matty had opened to a page and pointed to the unknown language. "It's called Greek," Leader said. "I can read a few words. But in the place of my childhood, we were not allowed to learn such things. So in my spare time, I have Mentor come and help me with languages. But . . ." Leader sighed. "I have so little spare time. Maybe when I'm old, I will sit here and study. I'd like that, I think."

Matty had replaced the book and run his hand gently over the leather bindings of the ones beside it.

"If you weren't allowed to learn," he asked, "why did they let you bring the books?"

Leader laughed. "You've seen the little sled," he said.

"In the Museum?"

"Yes. My vehicle of arrival. They've made such a thing of it, it's almost embarrassing. But it is true that I came on that sled. A desperate boy, half dead. No books! The books were brought to me later. I have never been as surprised in my life as I was the day those books arrived."

Matty had looked around at the thousands of books. In his own arms—and Matty was strong—he could have carried no more than ten or twelve at a time.

"How did they come to you?"

"A river barge. Suddenly there it was. Huge wooden crates aboard, and each one filled with books. Until that time I had always been afraid. A year had passed. Then two. But I was still afraid; I thought they would still be looking for me, that I would be recaptured, put to death, because no one had ever fled my community successfully before.

"It was only when I saw the books that I knew that things had changed, that I was free, and that back there, where I had come from, they were rebuilding themselves into something better.

"The books were a kind of forgiveness, I think."

"So you could have gone back," Matty said. "Was it too late? Had Forest given you Warnings?"

"No. But why would I go back? I had found a home here, the way everyone has. That's why we have the Museum, Matty, to remind us of how we came, and why: to start fresh, and begin a new place from what we had learned and carried from the old."

❧

Today Matty admired the books, as he always did in Leader's homeplace, but he didn't linger to touch or examine them. Nor did he stop to admire the staircase, with its intricate risers of crafted, polished wood that ascended in a circle to the next level.

When Leader called, "Up here, Matty," he bounded up the stairs to the second floor, into the spacious room where Leader lived and worked.

Leader was at his desk. He looked up from the papers in front of him and smiled at Matty. "How's the fishing?"

Matty shrugged and grinned. "Not too bad. Caught four yesterday."

Leader laid his pen aside and leaned back in his chair. "Tell me something, Matty. You and your friend are out there a lot, fishing. And you've been doing it for a long time—since you came to Village as a little boy. Isn't that so?"

"I don't remember exactly how long. I was only about this high when I came." Matty gestured with his hand, placing it level with the second button of his own shirt.

"Six years," Leader told him. "You arrived six years ago. So you've been fishing for all that time."

Matty nodded. But he stiffened. He was wary. It was too soon for his true name to be bestowed, he thought. Surely it was not going to be *Fisherman!* Was that why Leader had called him here?

Leader looked at him and began to laugh. "Relax, Matty! When you look like that, I can almost read your mind! Don't worry. It was only a question."

"A question about fishing. Fishing's a thing I do just to get food or to fool around. I don't want it to turn into something more." Matty liked that about Leader, that you could say what you wanted to him,

30

that you could tell him what you felt.

"I understand. You needn't worry about that. I was asking because I need to assess the food supply. Some are saying there are fewer fish than there once were. Look here, what I've been writing." He passed a paper over to Matty. There were columns of numbers, lists headed "Salmon" and "Trout."

Matty read the numbers and frowned. "It might be true," he said. "I remember at first I would pull fish after fish from the river. But you know what, Leader?"

"What?" Leader took the paper back from Matty and laid it with others on his desk.

"I was little then. And maybe you don't remember this, because you're older than I am . . ."

Leader smiled. "I'm still a young man, Matty. I remember being a boy." Matty thought he noticed a brief flicker of sadness in Leader's eyes, despite the warm smile. So many people in Village—including Matty—had sad memories of their childhoods.

"What I meant was, I remember all the fish, the feeling that they would never end. I felt that I could drop my line in again and again and again and there would always be fish. Now there aren't. But, Leader . . ."

Leader looked at him and waited.

"Things seem *more* when you're little. They seem bigger, and distances seem farther. The first time I came here through Forest? The journey seemed forever."

"It does take days, Matty, from where you started."

"Yes, I know. It still takes days. But now it doesn't seem as far or as long. Because I'm older, and bigger, and I've gone back and forth again and again, and I know the way, and I'm not scared. So it seems shorter."

Leader chuckled. "And the fish?"

"Well," Matty acknowledged, "there don't seem to be as many. But maybe it's just that I was a little boy back then, when the fish seemed endless."

Leader tapped the tip of his pen on the desk as he thought. "Maybe so," he said after a moment. He stood. From a table in the corner of the room he took a stack of folded papers.

"Messages?" Matty asked.

"Messages. I'm calling a meeting."

"About *fish?*"

"No. I wish it were just about fish. Fish would be easy."

Matty took the stack of message papers he would be delivering. Before he turned to the staircase to leave, he felt compelled to say, "Fish aren't ever easy. You have to use just the right bait, and know the right place to go, and then you have to pull the line up at just the right moment, because if you don't, the fish can wiggle right off your hook, and not everybody is good at it, and . . ."

He could hear Leader laughing, still, when he left.

❧

It took Matty most of the day to deliver all of the messages. It wasn't a hard task. He liked the harder ones better, actually, when he was outfitted with food and a carrying pack and sent on long journeys through Forest. Although he hadn't been sent to it in almost two years, Matty especially liked trips that took him back to his former home, where he could greet his boyhood pals with a somewhat superior smile, and snub those who had been cruel to him in the past. His mother was dead, he had been told. His brother was still there, and looked at Matty with more respect than he ever had in the past, but they were strangers to each other now. The community where he had lived was greatly changed and seemed foreign, though less harsh than he remembered.

Today he simply made his way around Village, delivering notice of the meeting that would be held the following week. Reading the message himself, he could understand Leader's questioning about the supply of fish, and the concern and worry that Matty had felt from him.

There had been a petition—signed by a substantial number of people—to close Village to outsiders. There would have to be a debate, and a vote.

It had happened before, such a petition.

"We voted it down just a year ago," the blind man reminded Matty when the message had been read to him. "There must be a stronger movement now."

"There are still plenty of fish," Matty pointed out, "and the fields are full of crops."

The blind man crumpled the message and dropped it into the fire. "It's not the fish or crops," he said. "They'll use that, of course. They argued dwindling food supply last time. It's . . ."

"Not enough housing?"

"More than that. I can't think of the word for it. *Selfishness,* I guess. It's creeping in."

Matty was startled. Village had been created out of the opposite: selflessness. He knew that from his studies and from hearing the history. Everyone did.

"But in the message—I could have read it to you again if you hadn't burned it—it says that the group who wants to close the border is headed by Mentor! The schoolteacher!"

The blind man sighed. "Give the soup a stir, would you, Matty?"

Obediently Matty moved the wooden ladle around in the pot and watched beans and chopped tomatoes churn in the thick mixture as it simmered. Thinking still of his teacher, he added, "He's not selfish!"

"I know he isn't. That's why it's puzzling."

"He welcomes everyone to the school, even new ones who have no learning, who can't even speak properly."

"Like you, when you came," the blind man said with a smile. "It couldn't have been easy, but he taught you."

"He had to tame me first," Matty acknowledged, grinning. "I was wild, wasn't I?"

Seer nodded. "Wild. But Mentor loves teaching those who need it."

"Why would he want to close the border?"

"Matty?"

"What?"

"Has Mentor traded, do you know?"

Matty thought about it. "It's school vacation now, so I don't see him as often. But I stop by his homeplace now and then . . ." He didn't mention Jean, the widowed schoolteacher's daughter. "I haven't noticed anything different in his household.

"No Gaming Machine," he added, laughing a little.

But the blind man didn't chuckle in reply. He sat thinking for a moment. Then he said, in a worried voice, "It's much more than just a Gaming Machine."

5

"The schoolteacher's daughter told me that her dog has three puppies. I can have one when it's big enough, if I like."

"Isn't she the one who promised you a kiss? Now a dog as well? I'd settle for the kiss if I were you, Matty." The blind man smiled, loosened a beet from the earth, and placed it in the basket of vegetables. They were in the garden together.

"I miss my dog. He wasn't any trouble." Matty glanced over to the corner of their homeplace's plot of land, beyond the garden, to the small grave where they had buried Branch two years before.

"You're right, Matty. Your little dog was a good companion for many years. It would be fun to have a puppy around." The blind man's voice was gentle.

"I could train a dog to lead you."

"I don't need leading. Could you train a dog to cook?"

"Anything but beets," Matty said, making a face as he threw another into the basket.

～

But when he went in the afternoon to the school-teacher's homeplace, Matty found Jean distraught. "Two died last night," she said. "They took sick. Now there's only one puppy left, and it's sick, and the mother as well."

"How have you tended them?"

Jean shook her head in despair. "Same as I would for my father or myself. Infusion of white willow bark. But the puppy's too little to drink, and the mother's too sick. She lapped a bit and then just put her head down."

"Will you take me to see them?"

Jean led him into the small house, and though he was concerned for the dogs, Matty found himself looking around as they walked through, remembering what the blind man had asked. He noticed the sturdy furniture, neatly arranged, and the bookcases filled with Mentor's books. In the kitchen, Jean's baking pans, and the bowls in which she mixed dough, were set out, ready for her wonderful breads to be made.

He saw nothing that hinted of a trade. Nothing silly like a Gaming Machine, nothing frivolous like the soft upholstered furniture decorated with fringe that a foolish young couple down the road had traded for.

Of course there were other kinds of trades, Matty knew, though he didn't fully understand. He had

37

heard murmurs about them. There were trades for things you didn't see. Those were the most dangerous trades.

"They're in here." Jean opened the door to the storage shed attached to the house at the back of the kitchen. Matty entered and knelt beside the mother dog where she lay on a folded blanket. The tiny puppy, motionless but for its labored breathing, lay in the curve of her belly, the way any puppy would. But a healthy pup would have been wiggling and sucking. This one should have been pawing at its mother for milk.

Matty knew dogs. He loved them. Gently he touched the puppy with his finger. Then, startled, he jerked his hand away. He had felt something painful.

Oddly, it made him think of lightning.

He remembered how he had been instructed, even as a small boy back in his old place, to go indoors during a thunderstorm. He had seen a tree split and blackened by a lightning strike, and he knew that it could happen to a human: the flash and the burning power that would surge through you, looking for a place to enter the earth.

He had watched through the window and seen great fiery bolts split the sky, and he had smelled the sulfurous smell that they sometimes left behind.

There was a man in Village, a farmer, who had stood in the field beside his plow, waiting as dark clouds gathered overhead, hoping the storm would pass by. The lightning had found him there, and though the farmer had survived, he had lost all his memory but for the sensation of raw power that had entered him that afternoon. People tended him now, and he helped with farm chores, but his energy was gone, taken away by the mysterious energy that lived in lightning.

Matty had felt this sensation—the one of pulsating power, as if he had the power of lightning within his own self—in the clearing, on a sunny day with no storm brewing.

He had tried to put it out of his mind afterward, any thoughts of the day it had happened, because it frightened him so and made him have a secret, which he did not want. But Matty knew, pulling his hand from the ailing puppy, that it was time to test it once again.

"Where's your father?" he asked Jean. He wanted no one to watch.

"He had a meeting to go to. You know about the petition?"

Matty nodded. Good. The schoolteacher was not around.

"I don't think he really even cares about the meeting. He just wants to see Stocktender's widow. He's courting her." Jean spoke with affectionate amusement. "Can you imagine? Courting, at his age?"

He needed the girl to be gone. Matty thought. "I want you to go to Herbalist's. Get yarrow."

"I have yarrow in my own garden! Right beside the door!" Jean replied.

He didn't need yarrow, not really. He needed her *gone*. Matty thought quickly. "Spearmint? Lemon balm? Catnip? Do you have all of those?"

She shook her head. "No catnip. If cats were attracted to my garden, the dog would make a terrible fuss.

"Wouldn't you, poor thing?" she said sweetly, leaning down to murmur to the dying mother dog. She stroked the dog's back but it did not lift its head. Its eyes were beginning to glaze.

"Go," Matty told her in an urgent voice. "Get those things."

"Do you think they'll help?" Jean asked dubiously. She took her hand from the dog and stood, but she lingered.

"Just go!" Matty ordered.

"You needn't use a rude tone, Matty," Jean said with an edge in her voice. But she turned with a flounce of her skirt and went. He barely heard the sound of the door closing behind her. Steeling himself against the painful vibrating shock that he knew would go through his entire body, Matty placed his left hand on the mother dog, his right on the puppy, and willed them to live.

∾

An hour later, Matty stumbled home, exhausted. Back at Mentor's house, Jean was feeding the mother dog and giggling at the antics of the lively puppy.

"Who would have thought of that combination of herbs? Isn't it amazing!" she had said in delight, watching the creatures revive.

"Lucky guess." He let Jean believe it was the herbs. She was distracted by the sudden liveliness of the dogs and didn't even notice how weak Matty was. He sat leaning against the wall in the shed and watched her tend them. But his vision was slightly blurred and his whole body ached.

Finally, when he had regained a little strength, he forced himself to stand and leave. Fortunately his own homeplace was empty. The blind man was out somewhere, and Matty was glad of that. Seer would have noticed something wrong. He could always feel it. He said the atmosphere in the homeplace changed, as if wind had shifted, if Matty had so much as a cold.

And this was much more. He staggered into his room off the kitchen and lay down on his bed, breathing hard. Matty had never felt so weak, so drained. Except for the frog . . .

The frog was smaller, he thought. But it was the same thing.

He had come across the little frog by chance, in the clearing. He had no reason to be there that day; he had simply wanted to be alone, away from busy Village, and had gone into Forest to get away, as he did sometimes.

41

Barefoot, he had stepped on the frog, and was star-tled. "Sorry!" he had said playfully, and reached down to pick the little fellow up. "Are you all right? You should have hopped away when you heard me coming."

But the frog wasn't all right, and couldn't have escaped with a hop. It hadn't been Matty's light step that had injured it; he could see that right away. Some creature—Matty thought probably a fox or weasel—had inflicted a terrible wound upon the small green thing, and the frog was almost dead of it. One leg dangled, torn away from the body, held there only by an oozing bit of ragged tissue. In his hand, the frog drew a shuddering breath and then was still.

"Someone chewed you up and spit you out," Matty said. He was sympathetic but matter-of-fact. The hard life and quick death of Forest's creatures were everyday things. "Well," he said, "I'll give you a nice burial."

He knelt to dig out a spot with his hands in the mossy earth. But when he tried to set the little body down, he found that he was connected to it in a way that made no sense. A painful kind of power surged from his hand, flowing into the frog, and held them bound together.

Confused and alarmed, he tried to scrape the sticky body of the frog off his hand. But he couldn't. The vibrating pain held them connected. Then, after a moment, while Matty knelt, still mystified by what was happening, the frog's body twitched.

"So you're not dead. Get off of me, then." Now he was able to drop the frog to the ground. The stab of pain eased.

"What was that all about?" Matty found himself talking to the frog as if it might be able to reply. "I thought you were dead, but you weren't. You're going to lose your leg, though. And your hopping days are over. I'm sorry for that."

He stood and looked down at the impassive frog. *Churrump.* Its throat made the sound.

"Yes. I agree. Same to you." Matty turned to leave. *Churrump.*

The sound compelled him to go back and to kneel again. The frog's wide-open eyes, which had been glazed with death only a few moments before, were now clear and alert. It stared at Matty.

"Look, I'm going to put you over here in the ferns, because if you stay in the open, some other creature will come along and gobble you up. You have a big disadvantage now, not being able to hop away. You'll have to learn to hide."

He picked up the frog and carried it to the thicket of high ferns. "If I had my knife with me," he told it, "I'd probably just slice through those threads that are holding your leg. Then maybe you could heal more quickly. As it is, you'll be dragging that leg around and it will burden you. But there's nothing I can do."

He leaned down to turn it loose, still thinking about how best to help it. "Maybe I can find a sharp rock and slice through. It's just a tiny bit of flesh and it probably wouldn't even pain you if I did it.

"You stay right here," Matty commanded, and placed the frog on the earth beside the ferns. *As if it could hop*, he thought.

Back at the edge of the small stream he had crossed, Matty found what he needed as a tool: a bit of rock with a sharp edge. He took it back to where the wounded frog lay, immobilized by its wound.

"Now," Matty told the frog, "don't be scared. I'm going to spread you out a bit and then carefully cut that dead leg away. It's the best thing for you." He turned the frog onto its back and touched the shredded leg, meaning to arrange it in a way that would make the amputation simple and fast. There were only a few sticky strands of flesh to slice through.

But he felt a sudden jolt of painful energy enter his arm, concentrated in his fingertips. Matty was unable to move. His hand grasped the nearly severed leg and he could feel his own blood moving through its vessels. His pulse thrummed and he could hear the sound of it.

Terrified, Matty held his breath for what seemed forever. Then it all stopped. The thing that had happened ended. He lifted his hand tentatively from the wounded frog.

Churrump.

Churrump.

"I'm leaving now. I don't know what happened, but I'm leaving now." He dropped the sharp rock and tried to rise, but his knees were weak and he felt dizzy and sick. Still kneeling beside the frog, Matty took a few long breaths, trying to get his strength again so that he could flee.

Churrump.

"Stop it. I don't want to hear that."

As if it understood what Matty had said, the frog turned, flopping itself over from its belly-up position, and moved toward the ferns. But it was not dragging a useless leg. Both legs were moving—awkwardly, to be sure, but the frog was propelling itself with both legs. It disappeared into the clump of quivering ferns.

After a moment Matty was able to stand. Desperately tired, he had made his way out of Forest and stumbled home.

∽

Now, lying on his bed, he felt the same exhaustion, magnified. His arms ached. Matty thought about what had happened. *The frog was very small. This was two dogs.*

This was bigger.

I must learn to control it, Matty told himself.

Then, surprisingly, he began to cry. Matty had a boyish pride in the fact that he never cried. But now he wept, and it felt as if the tears were cleansing him, as if his body needed to empty itself. Tears ran down his cheeks.

Finally, shuddering with exhaustion, he wiped his eyes, turned on his side, and slept, though it was still midday. The sun was high in the sky over Village. Matty dreamed of vague, frightening things connected to pain, and his body was tense even as he slept. Then his dream changed. His muscles relaxed and he became serene in his sleep. He was dreaming now of healed wounds, new life, and calm.

6

"New ones coming! And there's a pretty girl among them!"

Ramon called to Matty but didn't stop. He was hurrying past, eager to get to Village's entrance place, where new ones always came in. There was, in fact, a Welcome sign there, though many new ones, they had discovered, could not read. Matty had been one of those. The word welcome had meant nothing to him then.

"I saw it but couldn't read it," he had said to Seer once, "and you could have read it but you couldn't see it."

"We're quite a pair, aren't we? No wonder we get along so well together." The blind man had laughed.

"May I go? I'm almost done here." When Ramon ran past and called to them, Matty and the blind man had been clearing out the garden, pulling up the last of the overgrown pea vines. Their season was long past. Soon summer would end. They would be storing the root vegetables soon.

"Yes, of course. I'll go, too. It's important to welcome them."

They wiped their dirty hands quickly and left the garden, closing the gate behind them and following the same path Ramon had rushed along. The entrance was not far, and the new ones were gathered there. In the past, new ones had mostly arrived alone or in pairs, but now they seemed to come in groups: whole families, often, looking tired, for they had come great distances, and frightened, because they had left fearsome things behind and usually their escape had been dangerous and terrifying. But always they were hopeful, too, and clearly relieved to be greeted by the smiles. The people of Village prided themselves on the welcome, many of them leaving their regular work to go and be part of it.

Frequently the new ones were damaged. They hobbled on canes or were ill. Sometimes they were disfigured by wounds or simply because they had been born that way. Some were orphans. All of them were welcomed.

Matty joined the crowded semicircle and smiled encouragingly at the new ones as the greeters took their names, one by one, and assigned them to helpers who would lead them to their living spaces and help them settle in. He thought he saw the girl Ramon had mentioned, a thin but lovely girl about their age. Her face was dirty and her hair uncombed. She held the hand of a younger child whose eyes were thick with yellow mucus; it was a common ailment of new ones, quickly healed with herbal mixtures. He could tell that the girl was worried for the child,

48

and he tried to smile at her in a way that was reassuring.

There were more than usual this time. "It's a big group," Matty whispered to the blind man.

"Yes, I can hear that it is. I wonder if somehow they have begun to hear rumors that we may close."

As he spoke, they both heard something and turned. Approaching the welcoming entrance and the busy processing of the new ones, a small group of people Matty recognized—with Mentor leading them—came forward, chanting, "Close. Close. No more. No more."

The welcoming group was uncertain how to react. They continued to smile at the new ones and to reach forward to take their hands. But the chant made everyone uncomfortable.

Finally, in the confusion, Leader appeared. Someone had sent for him, apparently. The crowd parted to allow him through and the chanters fell silent.

Leader's voice was, as always, calm. He spoke first to the new ones, welcoming them. He would have done this later in the day, after they had been fed and settled. But now, instead of waiting, he reassured them briefly.

"We were all of us new ones once," he said with a smile, "except for the youngsters who have been born here.

"We know what you have been through.

"You will no longer be hungry. You will no longer

live under unfair rule. You will never be persecuted again.

"We are honored to have you among us. Welcome to your new home. Welcome to Village."

He turned to the greeters and said, "Do the processing later. They are tired. Take them to their living spaces so they can have baths and food. Let them rest for a while."

The greeters encircled the new ones and led them away.

Then Leader turned to those who remained. "Thank you, those of you who came to give welcome. It is one of the most important things we do in Village.

"Those of you who object? Mentor? You and the others?" He looked at the small group of dissenters. "You have that right, as you know. The right to dissent is one of our most important freedoms here.

"But the meeting is in four days. Let me suggest that instead of worrying and frightening these new ones, who have just come and are weary and confused, let us wait and see what the meeting decides.

"Even those of you who want to close Village to new ones—even you value the peace and kindness we have always embraced here. Mentor? You seem to be leading this. What do you say?"

Matty turned to look at Mentor, the teacher who meant so much to him. Mentor was thinking, and Matty was accustomed to seeing him deep in thought, for it was part of his classroom demeanor. He always thought over each question carefully, even the most foolish question from the youngest student.

Odd, Matty thought. The birthmark across Mentor's cheek seemed lighter. Ordinarily it was a deep red. Now it seemed merely pink, as if it were fading. But it was late summer. Probably, Matty decided, Mentor's skin had been tanned by the sun, as his own was; and this made the birthmark less visible.

Still, Matty was uneasy. Something *else* was different today about Mentor. He couldn't name the difference, not really. Was it that Mentor seemed slightly *taller?* How strange that would be, Matty thought. But the teacher had always walked with a bit of a stoop. His shoulders were hunched over. People said that he had aged terribly after his beloved wife's death, when Jean was just a small child. Sadness had done it.

Today he stood erect and his shoulders were straight. So he *seemed* taller, but wasn't, Matty decided with relief. It was simply a changed posture.

"Yes," Mentor said to Leader, "we will see what the meeting decides."

His voice sounded different, Matty noticed.

He saw that Leader, too, was noticing something about Mentor and was puzzled. But everyone was turning away now, the crowd dispersing, people returning to their usual daily tasks. Matty ran to catch up with the blind man, who had started walking the familiar path home.

Behind him he heard an announcement being made. "Don't forget!" someone was calling out. "Trade Mart tomorrow night!"

Trade Mart. With the other things that had consumed Matty's thoughts recently, he had almost forgotten about Trade Mart.

Now he decided he would attend.

∾

Trade Mart was a very old custom. No one remembered its beginnings. The blind man said that he had first known of it when he was a newcomer to Village, still an invalid with wounds to be tended. He had lain on a bed in the infirmary, in pain, unseeing, his memory slow to return, and half listened to the conversations of the gentle folk who took care of him.

"Did you go to the last Trade Mart?" he had heard one person ask another.

"No, I have nothing to trade. Did you?"

"Went and watched. It all seems foolishness to me."

He had put it from his mind, then. He had nothing to trade, either. He owned nothing. His torn, blood-stained clothes had been taken from him and replaced. From a cord around his neck dangled an amulet of some sort, and he felt its importance but could not remember why. Certainly he would not trade it for some trinket; it was all he had left of his past.

The blind man had described all of that to Matty.

"Later I went, just to watch," he told him.

Matty laughed at him. They were close, by then, and he could do that. *"Watch?"* he hooted.

The blind man laughed in reply. "I have my own kind of watching," he said.

"I know you do. That's why they call you Seer. You see more than most. Can anyone go to Trade Mart and watch?"

"Of course. There are no secrets here. But it was dull stuff, Matty. People called out what they wanted to trade for. Women wanted new bracelets, I remember, and they traded their old bracelets away. Things like that."

"So it's like Market Day."

"It seemed so to me. I never went back."

Now, speaking of it the evening of the new ones' arrival, the blind man expressed concern. "It's changed, Matty. I hear people talk of it now, and I feel the changes. Something's wrong."

"What kind of talk?"

The blind man was sitting with his instrument on his lap. He played one chord. Then he frowned. "I'm not sure. There's a secrecy to it now."

"I got up my nerve and asked Ramon what his parents traded for the Gaming Machine. But he didn't know. He said they wouldn't tell him, and his mother turned away when he asked, as if she had something to hide."

"I don't like the sound of it." The blind man stroked the strings and played two more chords.

"The sound of your own music?" Matty asked with a laugh, trying to lighten the conversation.

"Something's happening at Trade Mart," Seer said, ignoring Matty's attempt at humor.

"Leader said the same."

"He would know. I'd be wary of it, Matty, if I were you."

The next evening, while they prepared supper, he told the blind man he was planning to go.

"I know you said I was too young, Seer. But I'm not. Ramon's going. And maybe it's important for me to go. Maybe I can figure out what's happening."

Seer sighed and nodded. "Promise me one thing," he told Matty.

"I will."

"Make no trade. Watch and listen. But make no trade. Even if you're tempted."

"I promise." Then Matty laughed. "How could I? I have nothing to trade. What could I give for a Gaming Machine? A puppy too young to leave its mother? Who'd want that?"

The blind man stirred the chicken that simmered in a broth. "Ah, Matty, you have more than you know. And people will want what you have."

Matty thought. Seer was correct, of course. He had the thing that troubled him—the *power*, he thought of it—and perhaps there were those who would want it. Maybe he should find a way to trade it away. But the thought made him nervous. He turned his thoughts to other, less worrying things.

He had a fishing pole, but he needed that and loved it. He had a kite, stored in the loft, and perhaps one day he would trade it for a better kite.

But not tonight. Tonight he would only watch. He had promised the blind man.

7

It was early evening, just past supper, and others were hurrying, as Matty was, along the lane to the place where Trade Mart was held. He nodded to neighbors as he passed them, and waved to some he saw farther along. People nodded back or waved in reply, but there was none of the light-hearted banter that was ordinarily part of Village. There was an intentness to everyone, an odd seriousness, and a sense of worry—unusual in Village—pervaded the atmosphere.

No wonder Seer didn't want me to come, Matty thought as he approached. *It doesn't feel right.*

He could hear the noise. A murmur. People whispering to each other. It was not at all like Market Day, with its sounds of laughter, conversation, and commerce: good-natured bargaining, the squealing of pigs, the motherly cluck of hens with their cheeping broods. Tonight it was simply a low hum, a nervous whisper through the crowd.

Matty slipped into a group that had gathered and was standing nearest to the platform, a simple wooden structure like a stage that was used for many occasions when the people came together. The coming meeting to discuss the proposal to close Village would be held here, too, and Leader would stand on the stage to direct things and keep them orderly.

A large wooden roof covered the area so that rain would not prevent a gathering, and in the cold months the enclosing sides would be slid into place. Tonight, though, with the weather still warm, it was open to the evening. A breeze ruffled Matty's hair. He could smell the scent of the pine grove that bordered the area.

He found a place to stand next to Mentor, hoping that perhaps Jean would join her father, though she was nowhere to be seen. Mentor glanced down and smiled at him. "Matty!" he said. "It's a surprise to see you here. You've never been before."

"No," Matty said. "I have nothing to trade."

The schoolteacher put his arm affectionately over Matty's shoulders, and Matty noticed for the first time that the teacher had lost weight. "Ah," Mentor said, "you'd be surprised. Everyone has something to trade."

"Jean has her flowers," Matty said, hoping to turn the conversation to Mentor's daughter. "But she takes them to the market stall. She doesn't need Trade Mart for that.

"And," he added, "she already promised the puppy to me. She'd better not trade him away."

Mentor laughed. "No, the puppy is yours, Matty. And the sooner the better. He's full of mischief, and he chewed my shoes just this morning."

For a moment everything seemed as it had always been. The man was warm and cheerful, the same loving teacher and father he had been for years. His arm over Matty's shoulders was familiar.

But Matty found himself wondering suddenly why Mentor was there. Why, in fact, *any* of these people were here. None of them had brought any goods to trade. He looked around to confirm what he had noticed. People stood tensely, their arms folded or at their sides. Some of them were murmuring to one another. Matty noticed the young couple who were neighbors down the road from the house he shared with the blind man. They were conversing in low voices, perhaps arguing, and the young wife appeared worried at what her husband was saying. But their arms, too, like Matty's, like Mentor's, like everyone's, were empty. No one had brought anything to trade.

A silence fell and the crowd parted to make way for the tall, dark-haired man who was now striding toward the stage. He was called Trademaster. People said that he had come, already named, as a new one some years before, and had brought with him what he knew about trading from the place he had left. Matty had often seen him around Village and knew that he was in charge of Trade Mart and that he checked on things after, stopping at houses where trades had been made. He had come to Ramon's after his parents acquired the Gaming Machine. Tonight he carried nothing but a thick book that Matty had never seen before.

Mentor's arm fell from Matty's shoulders and the schoolteacher's attention turned eagerly toward the stage, where Trademaster was now standing.

"Trade Mart begins," Trademaster called. He had a loud voice with a slight accent, as many in Village had, the traces of their former languages lingering with them. The crowd fell absolutely silent now. Even the slightest whispering ceased. But over on the edge, Matty heard a woman begin to weep. He stood on tiptoe and peered toward her in time to see several people lead her away.

Mentor didn't even look toward the commotion of the weeping woman. Matty watched him. He noticed suddenly that Mentor's face looked slightly different, and he could not identify what the difference was. The evening light was dim.

More than that, the teacher, usually so calm, was now tense, alert, and appeared to be waiting for something.

"Who first?" Trademaster called, and while Matty watched, Mentor raised his hand and waved it frantically, like a schoolboy hoping for a reward. "Me! Me!" the schoolteacher called out in a demanding voice, and as Matty watched, Mentor shoved the people standing in front of him aside so that he would be noticed.

∾

Late that night, the blind man listened with a concerned look on his face while Matty described Trade Mart.

"Mentor was first, because he raised his hand so fast. And he completely forgot me, Seer. He had been standing with me and we were talking, just as we always have. Then, when they started, it was as if I didn't exist. He pushed ahead of everyone and went first."

"What do you mean, went first? Where did he go?"

"To the stage. He pushed through everyone. He shoved and jostled them aside, Seer. It was so odd. Then he went to the stage when Trademaster called his name."

The blind man rocked back and forth in his chair. Tonight he had not played music at all. Matty knew he was distressed.

"It used to be different. People just called out. There was a lot of laughter and teasing the time I went."

"No laughter tonight, Seer. Just silence, as if people were very nervous. It was a little scary."

"And what happened when Mentor got to the stage?"

Matty thought. It had been a little difficult to see through the crowd. "He just stood there. Then Trademaster asked him something, but it was as if he already knew the answer. And then everyone laughed a bit, as if they did, too, but it wasn't a having-fun

60

kind of laughter. It was a *knowing* kind."

"Could you hear what he asked?"

"I couldn't hear that first time, but I know what it was because he asked it of everyone who came up. It was the same each time. Just three words. *Trade for what?* That's what he asked each time."

"And was the answer the same from everyone?"

Matty shook his head, then remembered that he had to reply aloud. "No," he said. "It was different."

"Could you hear Mentor's reply?"

"Yes. It made everyone laugh in that odd way. Mentor said, 'Same as before.'"

The blind man frowned. "Did you get a feel for what that meant?"

"I think so, because everyone looked at Stocktender's widow, and she blushed. She was near me, so I could see it. Her friends poked at her, teasing, and I heard her say, 'He needs a few more trades first.'"

"Then what happened?"

Matty tried to remember the sequence of things. "Trademaster seemed to say yes, or at least to nod his head, and then he opened his book and wrote it in."

"I'd like to see that book," the blind man said, and then, laughing at himself, added, "or have you see it, and read it to me.

"What came next?"

"Mentor stood there. He seemed relieved that Trademaster had written something down for him."

"How could you tell?"

"He smiled and seemed less nervous."

"Then what?"

"Then everyone got very silent and Trademaster asked, 'Trade away what?' "

The blind man thought. "Another three words. Was it the same for each? The same 'Trade for what?' and then 'Trade away what?' "

"Yes. But each one said the answer to the first quite loudly, the way Mentor did, but they whispered the answer to the second, so no one could hear."

"So it became public, what they were trading for . . ."

"Yes, and sometimes the crowd called out in a scornful way. They *jeered*. I think that's the right word."

"And he wrote each down?"

"No. Ramon's mother went up, and when Trademaster asked, 'Trade for what?' she said, 'Fur jacket.' But Trademaster said no."

"Did he give a reason for the no?"

"He said she got a Gaming Machine already. Maybe another time, he said. Keep trying, he told her."

The blind man stirred restlessly in his chair. "Make us some tea, Matty, would you?"

Matty did so, going to the woodstove where the iron kettle was already simmering. He poured the water over tea leaves in two thick mugs and gave one to Seer.

"Tell me again the second three-word thing," the

62

blind man said after he had taken a sip.

Matty repeated it. "*'Trade away what?'*" He tried to make his voice loud and important, as Trademaster's had been. He tried to imitate the slight accent.

"But you couldn't hear any of the answers that people gave, is that right?"

"That's right. They whispered, and he wrote the whispers in his book."

Matty straightened in his chair with a sudden idea. "How about if I steal the book and read you what it says?"

"Matty, Matty . . ."

"Sorry," Matty replied immediately. Stealing had been so much a part of his previous existence that he sometimes still, even after years, forgot that it was not acceptable behavior in Village.

"Well," said the blind man after they had sipped their tea in silence for a moment, "I wish I could figure out what things people are trading away. You say they came empty-handed. Yet each one whispered something that was written down."

"Except for Ramon's mother," Matty reminded him. "Trademaster said no to her. But others got their trades. Mentor got his."

"But we don't know what."

"No. 'Same as before,' he asked for."

"Tell me this, Matty. When Mentor left the Trade Mart, he hadn't been given anything, had he? He wasn't carrying anything?"

"No. Nothing."

"Was anyone given anything to take away?"

"Some were told delivery times. Someone got a Gaming Machine.

"I'd really like a Gaming Machine, Seer," Matty added, though he knew it was hopeless.

But the blind man paid no attention to that. "One more question for you, Matty. Think hard about this."

"All right." Matty prepared himself to think hard.

"Try to remember if people *looked different* when it was over. Not everyone, but those who had made trades."

Matty sighed. It had been crowded, and long, and he had begun to be uncomfortable and tired by the time it ended. He had seen Ramon and waved, but Ramon was standing with his mother, who was angry at having been turned down by Trademaster. Ramon hadn't waved back.

He had looked for Jean, but she wasn't there.

"I can't remember. I wasn't paying attention by the end."

"What about the person who got a Gaming Machine? You told me someone did. Who was it?"

"That woman who lives over near the marketplace. You know the one? Her husband walks hunched over because he has a twisted back. He was with her but he didn't go up for a trade."

"Yes, I know who you mean. They're a nice family," the blind man said. "So she traded for a Gaming

Machine. Did you see her when she was leaving?"

"I think so. She was with some other women and they were laughing as they walked away."

"I thought you said she was with her husband."

"She was, but he walked behind."

"How did she seem?"

"Happy, because she got a Gaming Machine. She was telling her friends that they could come play with it."

"But anything else? Was there anything else about her that you remember, from *after* the trade, not before?"

Matty shrugged. He was beginning to be bored by the questioning. He was thinking about Jean, and that he might go to see her in the morning. Maybe his puppy would be ready. At least the puppy would be an excuse for a visit. It was healthy now, and growing fast, with big feet and ears; recently he had watched, laughing, when the mother dog had growled at it because it was nipping at her own ears in play.

Thinking of the puppy's behavior reminded Matty of something.

"Something *was* different," he said. "She's a nice woman, the one who got the Gaming Machine."

"Yes, she is. Gentle. Cheerful. Very loving to her husband."

"Well," said Matty slowly, "when she was leaving, walking and talking with the other women, and her husband behind trying to keep up, she whirled around suddenly and scolded him for being slow."

"Slow? But he's all twisted. He can't walk any other way," the blind man said in surprise.

"I know. But she made a sneering face at him and she imitated his way of walking. She made fun of him. It was only for a second, though."

Seer was silent, rocking. Matty picked up the empty mugs, took them to the sink, and rinsed them.

"It's late," the blind man said. "Time to go to bed." He rose from his chair and put his stringed instrument on the shelf where he kept it. He began to walk slowly to his sleeping room. "Good night, Matty," he said.

Then he said something else, almost to himself.

"So now she has a Gaming Machine," the blind man murmured. His voice sounded scornful.

Matty, at the sink, remembered something. "Mentor's birthmark is completely gone," he called to Seer.

8

The puppy was ready. So was Matty. The other little dog, the one who had been his childhood companion for years, had lived a happy, active life, died in his sleep, and had been buried with ceremony and sadness beyond the garden. For a long time Matty, missing Branch, had not wanted a new dog. But now it was time, and when Jean summoned him—her message was that Matty had to come right away to pick up the puppy, because her father was furious at its mischief—he hurried to her house.

He had not been to Mentor's homeplace since Trade Mart the previous week. The flower garden, as always, was thriving and well tended, with late roses in bloom and fall asters fat with bud. He found Jean there, kneeling by her flower bed, digging with a trowel. She smiled up at him, but it was not her usual saucy smile, fraught with flirtatiousness, the smile that drove Matty nearly mad. This morning she seemed troubled.

"He's shut in the shed," she told Matty, meaning the puppy. "Did you bring a rope to lead him home?"

"Don't need one. He'll follow me. I have a way with dogs."

Jean sighed, set her trowel aside, and wiped her forehead, leaving a smear of earth that Matty found very appealing. "I wish I did," she said. "I can't control him at all. He's grown so fast, and he's very strong and determined. My father is beside himself, wanting such a wild little thing gone."

Matty grinned. "Mentor deals with lots of wild little things in the schoolhouse. I myself was a wild little thing once, and it was he who tamed me."

Jean smiled at him. "I remember. What a ragged, naughty thing you were, Matty, when you came to Village."

"I called myself the Fiercest of the Fierce."

"You were that," Jean agreed with a laugh. "And now your puppy is."

"Is your father home?"

"No, he's off visiting Stocktender's widow, as usual," Jean said with a sigh.

"She's a nice woman."

Jean nodded. "She is. I like her. But, Matty . . ."

Matty, who had been standing, sat down on the grass at the edge of the garden. "What?"

"May I tell you something troubling?"

He felt himself awash with affection for Jean. He had for a long time been attracted to her girlish affectations, her silly charms and wiles. But now, for the first time, he felt something new. He perceived the young woman behind all those superficial things.

With her curly hair tumbling over her dirt-streaked forehead, she was the most beautiful person Matty had ever seen. And now she was talking to him in a way that was not foolish and childlike, designed to entrance, but instead was human and pained and adult. He felt suddenly that he loved her, and it was a feeling he had never known before.

"It's about my father," she said in a low voice.

"He's changing, isn't he?" Matty replied, startling himself, because he had not spelled it out in his mind before, had not said it aloud yet, yet here it was, and he was saying it to Jean. He felt an odd sense of relief.

Jean began to cry softly. "Yes," she said. "He has traded his deepest self."

"Traded?" That part took Matty by surprise because he had not thought it through to there. "Traded for what?" Matty asked in horror, and realized he was repeating the phrase from Trade Mart.

"For Stocktender's widow," she said, weeping. "He wanted her to love him, so he traded. He's becoming taller and straighter. The bald spot at the back of his head has grown over with hair, Matty. His birthmark has disappeared."

Of course. That was it. "I saw it," Matty told her, "but I didn't understand." He put his arm around the sobbing girl.

She caught her breath finally. "I didn't know how lonely he was, Matty. If I had known . . ."

"So that's why . . ." Matty was trying to sort through it in his head.

"The puppy. Once he would have loved a naughty puppy, Matty, the way he loved you when you were a raggedy boy. I knew it all for certain yesterday when he kicked the puppy. Till then I only suspected." Jean wiped her eyes with the back of her hand and left another endearing streak of dirt.

"And the petition!" Matty added, thinking of it suddenly.

"Yes. Father always welcomed new ones. It was the most wonderful part of Father, how he cared for everyone and tried to help them learn. But now . . ."

They heard a loud whimpering from the shed, and a scratching sound.

"Let him out, Jean, and I'll take him home before your father gets back."

She went to the shed door, opened it, and though her face was tear-streaked now, she smiled at the eager, ungainly puppy who bounded forth, jumped into Matty's arms, and licked his cheeks. The white tail was a whir.

"I need time to think," Matty said, subduing the puppy with a rhythmic scratch below his chin.

"What's to think about? There's nothing to be done. Trades are forever. Even if a stupid thing like a Gaming Machine breaks down, or if you tire of it—you don't get to reverse."

He wondered if he should tell her. She had seen the effect of his power on the puppy and its mother, but hadn't understood. Now, if he chose, perhaps he could explain. But he was uncertain about this. He did not know how far his power went and he did not want to promise this beloved girl something impossible. To repair a man's soul and deepest heart—to reverse an irreversible trade—might be far, far more than Matty could possibly undertake.

So he stayed silent, and took his lively puppy away.

❧

"Look! He sits now when I tell him to." Then Matty groaned and said, "Oh, sorry."

When would he ever learn to stop saying "Look" to a man who had no eyes?

But the blind man laughed. "I don't need to be able to look. I can hear that he sits. The sounds of his feet stop. And I don't feel his teeth on my shoes."

"He's smart, I think," Matty said optimistically.

"Yes, I think you're right. He's a good little puppy, Matty. He'll learn quickly. You don't need to worry about his mischief." The blind man reached out his hand and the puppy scampered to it and licked his fingers.

"And he's quite beautiful." In truth, Matty was trying to convince himself. The puppy was a combination of several colors, big feet, a whirligig of a tail, and lopsided ears.

"I'm sure he is."

"He'll need a name. I haven't thought of the right one yet."

"His true name will come to you."

71

"I hope I get my own soon," Matty said.

"It will come when the time comes."

Matty nodded and turned back to the dog. "First I thought of Survivor, because he was the only one of the puppies that did. But it's too long. It doesn't sound like the right one." Matty picked up the puppy and scratched its belly as it lay on his lap.

"So then . . ." Matty began to laugh. "Since he was the one that lived? I thought of Liver for a name."

"*Liver?*" The blind man laughed as well.

"I know, I know. It was a stupid idea. Liver with onions." Matty made a face.

He set the puppy on the floor again and it dashed off, tail wagging, to growl at the logs piled beside the stove and to chew at their edges where raw wood curled.

"You could ask Leader," the blind man suggested. "He's the one who gives true names to people. Maybe he'd do it for a puppy."

"That's a good idea. I have to go see Leader anyway. It's time to take messages around for the meeting. I'll take the puppy with me."

❧

Clumsy with his stubby legs and oversized feet, the puppy couldn't manage the stairs at Leader's homeplace. Matty picked him up and carried him, then set him on the floor in the upper room where Leader was waiting at his desk. The stacks of messages were ready. Matty could have taken them and left on his errand without pausing. But he lingered. He enjoyed Leader's company. There were things he wanted to tell him. He began to put them in order in his mind.

"Do you want to put a paper down for him?" Leader asked, watching with amusement as the little thing scampered about the room.

"No, he's fine. He never has an accident. It was the first thing he learned."

Leader leaned back in his chair and stretched. "He'll be good company for you, Matty, the way Branch was.

"Do you know," he went on, "in the place where I was a child, there were no dogs? No animals at all."

"No chickens? Or goats?"

"No, nothing."

"What did you eat, then?" Matty asked.

"We had fish. Lots of fish, from a hatchery. And plenty of vegetables. But no animal meat. And no pets at all. I never knew what it meant to have a pet. Or even to love something and be loved back."

His words made Matty think of Jean. He felt his face flush a little. "Did you never love a girl?" he asked.

He thought Leader would laugh. But instead the young man's face became reflective.

"I had a sister," Leader said, after a moment. "I think of her still, and hope she's happy."

He picked up a pencil from the desk, twirled it in his fingers, and gazed through the window. His clear

73

blue eyes seemed to be able to see great distances, even into the past, or perhaps the future.

Matty hesitated. Then he explained, "I meant a *girl*. Not like a sister. But a—well, a *girl*."

Leader put the pencil down and smiled. "I understand what you mean. There was a girl once, long ago. I was younger than you, Matty, but I was at the age when such things begin."

"What happened to her?"

"She changed. And I did too."

"Sometimes I think I want nothing to change, ever," Matty said with a sigh. Then he remembered what he had wanted to tell Leader.

"Leader, I went to Trade Mart," he said. "I hadn't been before."

Leader shrugged. "I wish they'd vote to end it," he said. "I never go anymore, but I did in the past. It seemed folly and time-wasting. Now it seems worse."

"It's the only way to get something like a Gaming Machine."

Leader made a face. "A Gaming Machine," he commented with disdain.

"Well, I'd like one," Matty grumbled. "But Seer says no."

The puppy wandered to a corner of the room, sniffed, made a circle of himself, collapsed, and fell asleep. Matty and Leader, together, watched it and smiled.

"It isn't just Gaming Machines and such." Matty had wondered how to say it, how to describe it.

Now, into the silence, as they watched the sleeping puppy, he found himself simply blurting it out. "Something else is happening at Trade Mart. People are changing, Leader. Mentor is."

"I've seen the changes in him," Leader acknowledged. "What are you telling me, Matty?"

"Mentor has traded away his deepest self," Matty said, "and I think that others are, too."

Leader leaned forward and listened intently as Matty described what he had seen, what he suspected, and what he knew.

∽

"Leader gave me a name for him, but I don't know if I like it."

Matty was back home by lunchtime, after delivering the last of the messages. The blind man was at the sink, washing some clothes.

"And what is it?" he asked, turning toward Matty's voice.

"Frolic."

"Hmmmm. It has a nice sound to it. How does the puppy feel about it?"

Matty lifted the puppy from where it had been riding, curled up inside his jacket. For most of the morning it had followed him, scampering at his heels, but eventually its short legs had tired, and Matty had carried it the rest of the way.

The puppy blinked—he had been asleep in the

jacket—and Matty set him on the floor.

"Frolic?" Matty said, and the puppy looked up His tail churned.

"*Sit, Frolic!*" Matty said. The puppy sat instantly. He looked intently at Matty.

"He did!" Matty told the blind man in delight.

"*Lie down, Frolic!*"

After a flicker of a pause, the puppy reluctantly sank to the floor and touched the rug with his small nose.

"He knows his true name already!" Matty knelt beside the puppy and stroked the little head. "Good puppy," he said. The big brown eyes gazed up at him and the spotted body, still sprawled obediently on the floor, quivered with affection.

"Good Frolic," Matty said.

9

There was much talk in Village about the coming meeting. Matty heard it everywhere, people arguing about the petition.

By now, some of the latest group of new ones were out and about, their sores clearing up, their clothes clean and hair combed, frightened faces eased, and their haunted, desperate attitudes changing to something more serene. Their children played, now, with other children of Village, racing down the lanes and paths in games of tag and hide-and-seek. Watching them, Matty remembered his own child self, his bravado and the terrible anguish it had concealed. He had not believed anyone would want him, ever, until he came to Village, and even then he had not trusted in its kindness for a long time.

With Frolic scampering at his heels, Matty made his way toward the marketplace to buy some bread.

"Good morning!" he called cheerfully to a woman he encountered on the path. She was one of the new ones, and he remembered her from the recent welcome. Her eyes had been wide in her gaunt face that day. She was scarred, as if by untended wounds, and one arm was held crookedly, so that it was awkward for her to do things.

But today she looked relaxed, and was making her unhurried way along the path. She smiled at Matty's greeting.

"Stop it, Frolic! *Down!*" Matty scolded his puppy, who had jumped to grab and tug at the frayed edge of the woman's skirt. Grudgingly Frolic obeyed him.

The woman leaned down to pat Frolic's head. "It's all right," she said softly. "I had a dog once. I had to leave him behind." She had a slight accent. Like so many of the people in Village, she had brought her way of speaking from her old place.

"Are you settling in?"

"Yes," she told him. "People are kind. They're patient with me. I've been injured, and I have to relearn some things. It will take time."

"Patience is important here, because we have so many in Village who have difficulties," Matty explained. "My father . . ."

He paused and corrected himself. "I mean the man I live with. He is called Seer. You've probably met him. He's blind. He strides around everywhere on the paths without a problem. But when he first arrived and had just lost his eyes . . ."

"I have a concern," the woman said suddenly, and he knew it was not a concern about the condition of the paths or directions to the buildings. He could see that she was worried.

"You can take any concern to Leader."

She shook her head. "Maybe you can answer. It's about the closing of Village. I hear talk of a petition."

"But you're already here!" Matty reassured her. "You needn't worry! You're part of us now. They won't send you away, even if they close Village."

"I brought my boy with me. Vladik. He's about your age. Maybe you've noticed him?"

Matty shook his head. He hadn't noticed the boy. There had been a large crowd of new ones. He wondered why the woman would be worried for her son. Perhaps he was having trouble adjusting to Village. Some new ones did. Matty himself had.

"When I came," he told her, "I was scared. Lonely, too, I think. And I behaved badly. I lied and stole. But look—now I am fine. I'm hoping to get my true name soon."

"No, no. My boy's a good boy," she said. "He doesn't lie or steal. And he's strong and eager. They have him working in the fields already. And soon he'll go to school."

"Well, then, no need to worry about him."

She shook her head. "No, I don't worry about him. It's my others. I brought Vladik but I had to leave my other children behind. We came first, my boy and I, to find the way. It was such a long, hard trip.

"The others are to come later. The little ones. My sister will bring them after I have made a place here."

Her voice faltered. "But now I hear people saying that the border will close. I don't know what to do. I think maybe I should go back. Leave Vladik here, to make a life, and go back to my little ones."

Matty hesitated. He didn't know what to say to her. Could she go back? She had been here only briefly, so it was not yet too late. Surely Forest would not entangle the poor woman yet. But if she did, what would she go back to? He didn't know how the woman had been injured. But he knew that in some places—it had been true, too, in Matty's old place—people were punished in terrible ways. He glanced at her scars, at her unset broken arm, and wondered if she had been stoned.

Of course she wanted to bring her children to the safety of Village.

"They'll be voting tomorrow," Matty explained. "You and I can't vote because we don't yet have our true names. But we can go and listen to the debate. We can speak if we want. And we can watch the vote."

He told her how to find the platform before which the people would gather. Using her good hand, the woman grasped Matty's hands with a warm gesture of thanks as she turned away.

At the market stall he bought a loaf of bread from Jean, who tucked a chrysanthemum blossom into the wrapping. She smiled at Frolic and leaned down to let him lick some crumbs from her fingers.

"Are you going to the meeting tomorrow?" he asked her.

"I suppose so. It's all my father talks about." Jean

sighed and began to rearrange her wares on the table.

"Once it was books and poetry," she said with sudden and passionate anguish. "I remember when I was small, after my mother died, he would tell me stories and recite poems at dinner. Then, later, he told me about the people who had written them.

"By the time we studied it in school—you remember, Matty, studying literature?—it was all so familiar to me, because of the way he had taught me when I didn't even know he was teaching."

Matty remembered. "He used different voices. Remember Lady Macbeth? *'Out, damn'd spot! Out, I say!'*" He tried to repeat the lines with the sinister yet regal voice Mentor had used.

Jean laughed. "And Macduff! I cried when my father recited Macduff's speech about the deaths of his wife and children."

Matty remembered that speech as well. Standing by the bakery stall with Frolic scampering about at their feet, Matty and Jean recited the lines together.

> *All my pretty ones?*
> *Did you say all? O hell-kite! All?*
> *What! all my pretty chickens and their dam*
> *At one fell swoop? . . .*
> *I cannot but remember such things were,*
> *That were most precious to me.*

Then Jean turned away. She continued restacking

the loaves on her table, but clearly her thoughts were someplace else. Finally she looked up at Matty and said in a puzzled voice, "It was so important to him, and he made it important to me: poetry, and language, and how we use it to remind ourselves of how our lives should be lived . . ."

Then her tone changed and became embittered. "Now he talks of nothing but Stocktender's widow, and of closing Village to new ones. What has happened to my father?"

Matty shook his head. He did not know the answer.

The recitation of Macduff's famous speech had reminded him of the woman he had spoken to on the path, the woman who feared for her lost children's future. *All my pretty ones.*

Suddenly he felt that they were all of them doomed.

He had forgotten completely about his own power. He had forgotten the frog.

10

The meeting to discuss and vote on the petition began in the orderly, careful way such meetings had always been handled. Leader stood on the platform, read the petition in his strong, clear voice, and opened the meeting to debate. One by one the people of Village stood and gave their opinions.

The new ones had come. Matty could see the woman he had met on the path, standing beside a tall, light-haired boy who must be Vladik. The two were with a group of new ones who had a place apart, since they could not vote.

Small children, bored, played along the edge of the pine grove. Matty had once been like them, when he was new here and hadn't liked meetings or debates. But now he stood with Seer and the other adults. He paid attention. He had not even brought Frolic, who usually accompanied Matty everywhere. Today the puppy was left at home, whimpering behind the closed door as they walked away.

It was frighteningly obvious now, with the population gathered, that something terrible was happening. At Trade Mart it had been evening, dark, and

Matty had been so interested in the proceedings that he had not noticed many individuals, only those who went to the platform, like Mentor, and the woman who had been so oddly cruel to her husband as they started home.

Now, though, it was bright daylight. Matty was able to watch everyone, and to his horror he could see the changes.

Near him stood his friend Ramon, with his parents and younger sister. It was Ramon's mother who had asked to trade for a fur jacket and been denied. But they had had a Gaming Machine for quite a while, and so a trade had been made in the past. Matty looked carefully at his friend's family. He had not seen Ramon since the day recently when he had suggested a fishing expedition and been told that Ramon was not well.

Ramon glanced at Matty and smiled. But Matty held his breath for a moment, dismayed to see that indeed his friend was ill. Ramon's face was no longer tanned and rosy-cheeked but instead seemed thin and gray. Beside him, his little sister seemed sick, too; her eyes were sunken and Matty could hear her cough.

Once, he knew, her mother would have leaned down to tend the little girl at the sound of such a cough. Now, while Matty watched, the woman simply shook the child roughly by a shoulder and said, "Shhhh."

One by one the people spoke, and one by one

Matty identified those who had traded. Some of those who had been among the most industrious, the kindest, and the most stalwart citizens of Village now went to the platform and shouted out their wish that the border be closed so that "we" (Matty shuddered at the use of "we") would not have to share the resources anymore.

We need all the fish for ourselves.

Our school is not big enough to teach their children, too; only our own.

They can't even speak right. We can't understand them.

They have too many needs. We don't want to take care of them.

And finally: *We've done it long enough.*

Now and then a lone citizen, untouched by trade, would go to the platform and try to speak. They spoke of the history of Village, how each of them there had fled poverty and cruelty and been welcomed at this new place that had taken them in.

The blind man spoke eloquently of the day he had been brought here half dead and been tended for months by the people of Village until, though he was still without sight, it had become his true home. Matty had been wondering whether he, too, would go up and speak. He wanted to, for surely Village had also become his true home, and saved him, but he felt a little shy. Then he heard the blind man begin to speak on his behalf:

"My boy came here six years ago as a child. Many of you remember the Matty he was then. He fought and swore and stole."

Matty liked the sound of the phrase "my boy," which he had never heard the blind man use before. But he was embarrassed to see people turn and look at him.

"Village changed him and made him what he is now," the blind man said. "He will receive his true name soon."

For a moment Matty hoped that Leader, who was still standing on the platform, would hold up his hand to call for silence, would call Matty, place his hand on Matty's forehead, then announce the true name. It happened that way, sometimes.

Messenger. Matty held his breath, hoping for that.

But instead he heard another voice, not Leader's.

"I remember what he was like! If we close the border, we won't have to do that anymore! We won't have to deal with thieves and braggarts and people who have lice in their hair, the way Matty did then, when he came!"

Matty turned to look. It was a woman. He was stunned, as if someone had slapped him. It was his own neighbor, the very woman who had made clothes for him when he came. He remembered standing there in his rags while she measured him and then put on her thimble to stitch the clothing for him. She had a soft voice then, and talked gently to him while she sewed.

Now she had a sewing machine, a very fancy one, and bolts of fabric with which she created fine clothing. Now the blind man stitched the simple things that he and Matty needed.

So she, too, had traded, and was turning not only on him, but on all new ones.

Her voice incited others, and now large numbers of people were calling out, "Close Village! Close the border!"

Matty had never seen Leader look so sad.

❧

When it was over, and the vote to close Village had been finalized, Matty trudged home beside the blind man. At first they were silent. There was nothing to be said. Their world had changed now.

After a bit Matty tried to talk, to be cheerful, to make the best of things.

"I suppose he'll send me out now to all the other villages and communities with the message. I'll be doing a lot of traveling. I'm glad it isn't winter yet. It's hard in snow."

"He came in snow," the blind man said. "He knows what it's like."

Matty wondered for a moment what he was talking about. Who? *Oh yes,* he thought. *The little sled.*

"Leader knows better than anyone about things," Matty remarked. "And he's still younger than many."

"He sees beyond," Seer said.

"What?"

"He has a special gift. Some people do. Leader sees beyond."

Matty was startled. He had noticed the quality of Leader's pale blue eyes, how they seemed to have a kind of vision most people didn't have. But he had not heard it described that way before.

It made him think of what he had only recently come to know about himself.

"So some people, like Leader, have a special gift?"

"It's true," Seer replied.

"Is it always the same? Is it always—what did you say?—seeing beyond?"

They were nearing the curve in the path where it branched off and led to their homeplace. Matty watched in awe, as he always did, how the blind man felt the coming curve and knew even in his darkness where to turn.

"No. It's different for different people."

"Do you have it? Is that how you know where to walk?"

The blind man laughed. "No. I've learned that. I've been without eyes for many years. At first I stumbled and bumped into things. People had to help me all the time. Of course in the old days in Village, people were quick to help and guide."

His voice became bitter. "Who knows what will happen now?"

They had arrived at the house and could hear Frolic

scratching at the door and woofing in excitement at the sound of their approach.

Matty didn't want the conversation to end here. He wanted to tell the blind man about himself, about his secret.

"So you don't have a special gift, like Leader, but other people do?"

"My daughter does. She told me of it that night, the night you took me to her."

"Kira? She has a special gift?"

"Yes, your old friend Kira. The one who taught you manners."

Matty ignored that. "She must be all grown up now. I saw her last time I was there, but it's been almost two years. But, Seer, what do you mean . . ."

The blind man stopped unexpectedly on the steps leading to the door. "*Matty!*" he said with sudden urgency.

"What?"

"I've just realized. The border will be closing in three weeks."

"Yes."

Seer sat down on the steps. He put his head in his hands. Sometimes he did that when he was thinking. Matty sat beside him and waited. He could hear Frolic inside, throwing himself against the door in frustration.

Finally the blind man spoke. "I want you to go to your old village, Matty. Leader will be sending you anyway, with the message.

"He'll no doubt send you to several places. But, Matty, I want you to go to your old village first. Leader will understand."

"But I don't."

"My daughter. She said some day she would come here to live, when the time was right. You know her, Matty. You know she had things to accomplish there first."

"Yes. And she has, Seer. I could tell when I was last there. Things have changed. People take good care of their children now. And . . ."

He hesitated, unable to speak for a moment, because the memory of his own abuse had returned. Then he added simply, "Kira made things change. Things are better now."

"There are only three weeks left, Matty. After the border closes it will be too late. She won't be allowed to come. You must bring her here before that happens.

"If you don't, Matty, I will never see her again."

"It always seems strange to me when you say 'see.'"

The blind man smiled. "I see in my heart, Matty."

Matty nodded. "I know you do. I'll bring her to you. I'll leave here tomorrow."

Together they rose. Evening was coming. Matty opened the door and Frolic leaped into his arms.

11

"Tuck it inside your shirt, Matty, so it won't get rumpled. You have a long journey ahead."

Matty took the packet of folded messages in the thick envelope, and placed it where Leader indicated, inside his shirt next to his chest. He didn't say so to Leader, but he thought that later, when he gathered his traveling things, he would probably find a different place for the envelope. He would put it with his food supplies and blanket. It was true that here, inside his shirt, was the safest and cleanest place. But he had planned to carry Frolic there, against his chest.

There was not time, in three weeks, to make journeys to all the other places and communities. Some of them were many days away, and a few places could be reached only by riverboat. Matty was not qualified to go by river; the man called Boater was always the one who took messages and trading goods by that route.

But it had been decided that the message would be posted on every path throughout Forest, so that any new ones coming would see it and turn back. Matty was the only one who knew all the paths, who was not afraid to enter Forest and travel in that dangerous place. He would post the messages there. And he would go on to his own old place as well. There had been ongoing communication between that place and Village for years; now they must be told of the new ruling.

Leader was standing now at the window, as he so often did, looking down at Village and the people below. Matty waited. He was in a hurry to be off, to begin his long journey, but he had a feeling there was something that Leader wanted to tell him, something still unsaid.

Finally Leader turned to Matty, standing beside him. "He's told you that I see beyond, hasn't he?"

"Yes. He says you have a special gift. His daughter does, too."

"His daughter. That would be the girl called Kira, the one who helped you leave your old place. He never talks about her."

"It makes him too sad. But he thinks about her all the time."

"And you say she has a gift, too?"

"Yes. But hers is different. Each gift is different, Seer said."

Do you know about mine? Matty thought. But he did not need to ask.

As if he had read Matty's mind, Leader told him, "I know of yours."

Matty shuddered. The gift still frightened him so.

"I kept it secret," he said apologetically. "I haven't even told Seer. I didn't want to be secretive. But I'm still trying to understand it. I try to put it out of my mind. I try to forget that it's there inside me. But then it just appears. I can feel it coming. I don't know how to stop it."

"Don't try. If it comes without your summoning it, it is because of need. Because someone needs your gift."

"A *frog*? It was a frog first!"

"It was to show you. It always starts with a small thing. For me? The very first time I saw beyond? It was an apple."

Despite the solemnity of the conversation, Matty chuckled. A frog and an apple. *And a puppy,* he realized.

"Wait for the true need, Matty. Don't spend the gift."

"But how will I know?"

Leader smiled. He rubbed Matty's shoulder affectionately. "You'll know," he said.

Matty looked around for Frolic and saw that he was curled in the corner, asleep. "I should go. I haven't packed my things yet. And I want to stop by and tell Jean I'm going, so she won't wonder where I am."

Leader kept him there within the comfortable curve of his arm. "Matty, wait," he said. "I want to . . ." Then he gazed through the window again. Matty stood there, wondering what he was to wait for.

Then he felt something. The weight of the young man's arm took on a quality of something beyond human flesh. It came alive with power. Matty felt it from the arm, but he knew, as well, that it was pervading all of Leader's being. He understood that it was Leader's gift at work.

Finally, after what seemed an unendurable few moments, Leader lifted his arm away from Matty. He exhaled. His body sagged slightly. Matty helped him to a chair and he sat there, exhausted, breathing hard.

"Forest is thickening," Leader said when he could speak.

Matty didn't know what he meant. It sounded ominous. But when he looked through the window, to the row of underbrush and pines that was the border of Forest, it looked no different to him.

"I don't understand it exactly," Leader said. "But I can see a thickening to Forest, like a . . ." He hesitated.

"I was going to say like a clotting of blood. Things turning sluggish and sick."

Matty looked through the window again. "The trees are just the same, Leader. There's a storm coming, though. You can hear the wind. And look. The sky is turning dark. Maybe that's what you saw."

Leader shook his head skeptically. "No. It was Forest I saw. I'm sure. It's hard to describe, Matty, but I was trying to look *through* Forest in order to get a feeling for Seer's daughter. And it was very, very hard to push through. It was—well, *thick*.

"I think you had better not go, Matty. I'm sorry. I know you love making your journeys, and that you take pride in being the only one who can. But I think there may be danger in Forest this time."

Matty's heart sank. He had hoped to be given his true name, Messenger, because of this trip. At the same time, something told him that Leader might be right.

Then he remembered. "Leader, I *have* to!"

"No. We can post the messages at the entrance to Village. It will mean new ones will have to turn back after terribly long journeys, and that's tragic. But—"

"No, it's not the messages! It's Seer's daughter! I promised him I would go and bring Kira home. It will be her last chance to come. His last chance to be with her."

"And she will want to come?"

"I'm sure she will. She always intended to someday. And she has no family there. She's old enough to marry, but no one would want her. Her leg is crooked. She walks with a stick."

Leader took several deep breaths. "Matty," he said, "I'm going to try again to see beyond Forest. I'm going to try to see Seer's daughter and her needs. You may stay with me now, because whether you make this journey will depend on what I learn. But be aware that it is very hard for me to do this twice in a row. Don't be distressed as you watch."

He stood again and went to the window. Matty,

knowing he could be of no help, went to the corner where Frolic was asleep and sat down beside his puppy. From there he watched Leader's body tense, as if he were in pain. He heard Leader gasp and then moan slightly.

The young man's blue eyes remained open but no longer seemed to be looking at the ordinary things in the room or through the window. He had gone, eyes and whole being, far into a place that Matty could not perceive and where no one could follow him.

He seemed to shimmer.

Finally he slumped into the chair, shaking, and tried to catch his breath.

Matty went to him, stood beside him, and waited while Leader rested. He remembered how he felt after he had healed the puppy and its mother. He remembered the desperate need to sleep.

"I reached where she is," Leader said when he could speak again.

"Did she know you were there? Could she feel you there?"

Leader shook his head. "No. To make her aware of me would have taken more energy than I had. It's so very far, and Forest is so thick now, to go through."

Matty had a sudden thought. "Leader? Do you think two gifts could *meet?*"

Leader, still breathing hard, stared at him. "What do you mean?"

"I'm not sure. But what if you could go halfway— and she could, too? So you could meet in the middle with your gifts? It wouldn't be so hard if you only went halfway. If you *met*."

Leader's eyes were closed, now. "I don't know, Matty," he said.

Matty waited but Leader said nothing more, and after a while Matty feared he was asleep. "Frolic?" he called, and the puppy woke, stirred, and came to him.

"Leader," Matty said, leaning close to him, "I'm going to go. I'm going to get the blind man's daughter."

"Be very careful," Leader murmured. His eyes were closed. "It is dangerous now."

"I will. I always am."

"Don't waste your gift. Don't spend it."

"I won't," Matty replied, though he was not certain what the words meant.

"Matty?"

"Yes?" He was at the top of the stairs now, holding Frolic, who still couldn't manage the staircase on his own.

"She's quite lovely, isn't she?"

Matty shrugged. He understood that Leader was referring to Kira but the blind man's daughter was older than he. She had been like a big sister to him. No one in the old place had thought her lovely. They had been contemptuous of her weakness.

"She has a crooked leg," Matty reminded Leader. "She leans on a stick to walk."

"Yes," Leader said. "She's very lovely." But his

voice was hard to hear now, and in a second he was asleep. Matty, holding Frolic, hurried down the stairs.

❦

It was late in the day by the time Matty was ready to go. It had rained heavily, and though the rain had stopped, wind still blew, and the leaves of the trees fluttered and revealed their pale undersides. The sky was dark, from the storm and from the approach of evening.

He placed the packet of messages inside his rolled blanket. By the sink, the blind man was putting food into Matty's backpack. He could not carry enough for the entire journey; it was too long. But Matty was accustomed to living on the food that Forest provided. He would feed himself along the way when what Seer packed was gone.

"While you're away, I'll be fixing the spare room for her. Tell her that, Matty. She'll have a comfortable place to live. And she can have a garden. I know that's important to her. She's never been without a garden."

"I won't need to convince her. She's always said she'd come when the time was right. Now it is. Leader could tell. So she'll know, too. You said she has a gift." Matty, folding a sweater, tried to reassure the blind man.

"It's hard to leave the only place you've known."

"You did it," Matty reminded him.

"I had no choice. I was brought here when they found me in Forest with my eyes gone."

"Well, I did it. Many have."

"Yes. That's true. But I hope it won't be hard for her."

Matty glanced over. "Don't put those beets in. I hate beets."

"They're good for you."

"Not if they're thrown on the ground. And that's what they'll be if you put them in."

The blind man chuckled and dropped the beets into the sink. "Well," he said, "they're heavy anyway. They'd weigh you down. But I'm putting carrots in."

"Anything but beets."

There was a knock on the door, and it was Jean, her hair curlier than usual from the dampness that remained after the rain. "Are you still going, Matty, in this weather?"

Matty laughed at her concern. "I've gone through Forest in snow," he boasted. "This weather is nothing. Yes, I'm about to leave. I'm just packing food."

"I've brought you some bread," she said, and took the wrapped loaf from the basket she carried. He noticed that she had decorated it with a leafy sprig and a yellow chrysanthemum blossom.

Matty took the loaf and thanked her, though secretly he wondered how he would ever fit it in. Finally the blind man found a way to tuck it inside the rolled blanket.

"I want to stop on my way out of Village and see Ramon," Matty said. "I'd better hurry or I'll never get started."

"Oh, Matty," Jean said. "You don't know? Ramon's very sick. His sister, too. They've put a sign on the door to their house. No one can enter."

Troubling though the news was, Matty was not surprised. Ramon had been coughing, feverish-looking, and increasingly unwell for days now. "What does Herbalist say?"

"That's why they put the sign up. Herbalist is afraid it may be contagious. That an epidemic could come."

What was happening to Village? Matty felt a terrible unease. There had never been an epidemic here. He remembered the place he had come from, where many had died, from time to time, and all of their belongings had been burned, after, in hopes of destroying the illnesses carried by filth or fleas or, some thought, sorcery. But it had never happened here. People had always been so careful here, so clean.

He could see that the blind man's face had taken on a worried look, too, at the news.

For a moment, Matty stood there thinking while Seer arranged his pack on his back and attached the rolled blanket below it. He thought of the frog first, then the puppy, and wondered if his gift could save his friend. He could go to Ramon's house now, and place his hands upon the feverish body. He knew it would be indescribably hard, would take all of his strength, but he thought there might be a chance.

But what then? If he himself survived such an attempt, he would be desperately weakened, he knew, and would have to recover. He could not possibly make the journey through Forest if he first weakened himself on Ramon's behalf. Forest was already thickening, he knew, whatever that meant. It would soon become impassable. The blind man's daughter would be lost to them forever.

And, most important, Leader had told him to save his gift. *Don't spend it,* Leader had said.

So Matty decided with regret that he would have to leave Ramon to his illness.

"Look," Jean said suddenly. "Look at this. It's *different.*"

Matty glanced over and saw that she was standing in front of the tapestry Kira had made for her father. Even from where he stood, he could see what Jean meant. The entire forest area, the hundreds of tiny stitches in shades of green, had darkened, and the threads had knotted and twisted in odd ways. The peaceful scene had changed into something no longer beautiful. It had an ominous feel to it, a feel of impenetrability.

He went near to it and stared at it, puzzled and alarmed.

"What is it, Matty?" Jean asked.

"Nothing. It's all right." He indicated with his eyes that she should not speak aloud of the odd change in the tapestry. Matty did not want Seer to know.

It was time to go.

He wriggled his shoulders to adjust the pack comfortably on his back, and leaned forward to hug the blind man, who murmured to him, "Be safe."

To his surprise, Jean kissed him. So often in the past, teasing, she had said she would, one day. Now she did, and it was a quick and fragrant touch to his lips that gave him courage and, even before he started out, made him yearn to come back home.

12

Frolic was afraid of the dark. Matty had never noticed it before, because always they had been indoors, with the oil lamp glowing, at night. He laughed a little to hear the puppy whimper in fear when night fell and Forest turned black. He picked him up and murmured words of reassurance but could feel the dog's body tremble, still, in his arms.

Well, thought Matty, it was time to sleep, anyway. He was quite near the clearing where the frog had been and perhaps still was. Carefully he made his way across the soft moss, holding Frolic against his chest and feeling the way with his feet. Then he knelt in the gnarled root bed of a tall tree and removed his pack. He unrolled the blanket, fed Frolic a few pieces torn from the loaf of bread, nibbled at it himself, and then curled up with his puppy and drifted off.

Churrump.
Churrump.
Frolic raised his head. His nose twitched and he flicked his ears curiously at the sound. But then he buried his head again under the curve of Matty's arm. Soon he too slept.

The days of the journey passed, and after the fourth night, the food was gone. But Matty was strong and unafraid, and to his surprise, little Frolic did not need to be carried. The puppy followed him and sat watching patiently as he posted the messages along divergent paths. Doing so lengthened the journey considerably. If he had gone straight through, he would be approaching Kira's village, his own home in the past, quite soon. But he reminded himself that being a messenger was his most important task, and so he took the side paths, walked great distances, and left the message of Village's closure at each place where new ones coming could be advised to turn back.

The scarred woman and her group had come from the east, he knew. There was a look that identified the easterners. He could see, on the path to the east, remaining bits of evidence that they had come through not long before: crushed underbrush where they had huddled to sleep, chunks of charcoal where a fire had been, a pink ribbon that had fallen, Matty thought, from a child's hair. He picked it up and put it in his backpack.

He wondered if the woman had left her son behind and returned alone to her other children by now. There was no sign of her.

The weather remained clear and he was grateful for that, because although he had bragged about past journeys through snow, in truth it was very hard to fight the elements, and almost impossible to find food in bad weather. Now there were early-fall berries and many nuts; he laughed at the chattering squirrels who were storing their own provisions, and with little guilt robbed a nest he found that was half filled with winter fare.

He knew places to fish, and the best way to catch them. Frolic turned up his nose at fish, even after Matty had grilled one on his small fire.

"Go hungry, then," Matty told him, laughing, and finished the browned, glistening fish himself. Then, as he watched, Frolic cocked his ears, listening, and dashed off. Matty heard a squawk, then a flurry of wings and rustling leaves and growls. After a bit, Frolic returned, looking satisfied, and with a bit of feather stuck to his whiskers.

"So? I had fish, you had bird." It amused Matty to talk to Frolic as if he were human. Since his other puppy had died, he had always traveled the paths alone. Now it was a treat to have company, and sometimes he felt that Frolic understood every word he said.

Although it was a subtle change, he understood what Leader had meant when he said that Forest was thickening. Matty knew Forest so well that he could anticipate changes that came with the seasons. Ordinarily, at summer's end, as now, some leaves would be falling, and by the time snow came, later, many trees would be bare. In the heart of winter, he needed to find water at the places where streams rushed quickly and didn't freeze; many of the quiet pools he knew well would be coated with ice. In spring there would be irritating insects to brush from his face, but there would be fresh, sweet berries then, too.

Always, though, it was familiar.

But on this journey, something was different. For the first time, Matty felt hostility from Forest. The fish were slow to come to his hook. A chipmunk, usually an amiable companion, chittered angrily and bit his finger when he held his hand toward it. Many red berries, of a kind he had always eaten, had black spots on them and tasted bitter; and for the first time he noticed poison ivy growing across the path again and again, where it had never grown before.

It was darker, too. The trees seemed to have moved at their tops, leaning toward each other to create a roof across the path; they would protect him from rain, he realized, and perhaps that was a good thing. But they didn't seem benevolent. They created darkness in the middle of day, and shadows that distorted the path and made him stumble from time to time on roots and rocks.

And it smelled bad. There was a stench to Forest now, as if it concealed dead, decaying things in the new thick darkness.

Camping in a clearing that he knew well from previous journeys, Matty sat on a log that he had often used as a seat while he cooked his meal. Suddenly it crumbled under him, and he had to pick himself up and brush rotting bark and slimy, foul-smelling material from his clothing. The piece of log that had been there so long, sturdy and useful, had simply fallen into chunks of dead vegetative matter; never again would it provide Matty a place to rest. He kicked it away and watched countless dislodged beetles scurry to new hiding places.

He began to have trouble sleeping. Nightmares tormented him. His head ached suddenly, and his throat was sore.

But he was not far, now, from his destination. So he trudged on. To divert himself from the discomfort that Forest had become, he thought about himself as a little boy. He remembered his earliest days when he had called himself the Fiercest of the Fierce, and his friendship then with the girl named Kira who was the blind man's daughter.

13

Such a swaggering, brash little boy he had been! With no father, and only an impoverished, embittered mother to try to make a life for children she had not wanted and did not love, Matty had turned to a life of small crimes and spirited mischief. Most of his time had been spent with a ragtag band of dirty-faced boys who carried out whatever schemes they could to survive. The harshness of his homeplace led him to thievery and deceit; had he been grown, he would have been imprisoned or worse.

But there had always been a gentle side to Matty, even when he had disguised it. He had loved his dog, a mongrel he had found injured and had nursed back to health. And he had come, eventually, to love the crippled girl called Kira, who had never known her father, and whose mother had died suddenly and left her alone.

"Mascot," Kira had called him, laughing. "Sidekick." She had made him wash, taught him manners, and told him stories.

"I be the Fiercest of the Fierce!" he had bragged to her once.

"You are the dirtiest of the dirty faces," she had said, laughing, in reply, and given him the first bath he ever had. He had struggled and protested, but in truth had loved the feel of warm water. He had never learned to love soap, though Kira gave him some for his own. But he felt the years of grime slip from him and knew that he could turn into someone cleaner, better.

Roaming as he always had, Matty had learned the intricate paths of Forest. One day he had found his way to Village for the first time, and had met the blind man there.

"She lives?" the blind man had asked him, unbelieving. "My daughter is alive?"

It was very dangerous for the blind man to return. Those who had tried to kill him, who had left him for dead years before, thought they had succeeded. They would have slain him instantly had he found his way back. But Matty, a master of stealth, had brought him secretly, at night, to meet his daughter for the first time. He watched from a corner of the room as Kira recognized the broken stone that Seer wore as an amulet, and matched it to her own, fitting it to the fragment given to her by her dying mother. Matty saw the blind man touch his daughter's face, to learn her, and he watched in silence as they mourned Kira's mother together, their hearts connected by the loss.

Then, when darkness came the next night, he had led the blind man back again. But Kira would not come. Not then.

"Someday," she had told Matty and her father when they begged her to return with them to Village. "I'll come someday. There's time still. And I have things to do here first."

"I suppose there's a young man," the blind man had said to Matty as they traveled back without her. "She's the age for it."

"Nah," Matty had said scornfully. "Not Kira. She has better stuff on her mind.

"Anyways," he had added, referring to her twisted leg, "she has that horrid gimp. No one can marry iffen they got a gimp. She's lucky they didn't feed her to the beasts. They wanted to. They only kept her 'cause she could do things they needed."

"What things?"

"She grows flowers, and—"

"Her mother did, too."

"Yes, her mum taught her, and to make the colors from them."

"Dyes?"

"Yes, she dyes the threads and then she makes pictures from them. No one else can do it. She has like a magic touch, they say. And they want her for that."

"She would be honored in Village. Not only for her talent but for her twisted leg."

"Turn here." Matty took the blind man's arm and guided him to the right side of a turning in the path. "Watch the roots there." He noticed that a root lifted itself and stabbed slightly at the man's sandaled foot. It made him very nervous, guiding on this

110

return trip, because he could feel, being familiar with it, that Forest was giving small Warnings to the blind man. He would not be allowed to come through again.

"She'll come when she's ready," he reassured Kira's father. "And till then, I'll go back and forth between."

But it had been two years since he had last seen Kira.

∾

Matty emerged from Forest with a stumble, blinking at the sudden sunshine, for he had been in the dim thickness of trees for many days now and felt that he had almost forgotten light.

He fell on the path and sat there panting, slightly dizzy, with Frolic pawing worriedly at his leg. In the past he had always—what would the word be? *strolled*—from Forest, sometimes whistling. But this was different. He felt that he had been expelled. Chewed up and spat out. When he looked back toward the trees, in the direction he had come, it seemed inhospitable, unwelcoming, locked down.

He knew he would have to reenter Forest and return by those same dark paths that now seemed so ominous. He would have to lead Kira through, to the safety of her future with her father. And he knew suddenly that it would be his last journey in that place.

There was not much time left, and he would not be

able to linger here, to look up his boyhood pals, to reminisce with them about their pranks, or to brag a little about his status now. He usually did that when he came. He would not even have time to say good-bye to the stranger his brother had become.

Village would close in three weeks from the time of the proclamation. Matty had calculated very carefully. He had counted the days of his journey, adding in the extra days it took for his side trips to tack the messages in place. Now he had just enough time to rest, which he badly needed to do, collect food for the return journey, and persuade Kira to come with him. If they moved steadily and without interruption through Forest (though he knew it would be slower with the girl, who had to lean on her stick) they would arrive in time.

Matty blinked, took a deep breath, got to his feet, and hurried on to the small cottage around the next turning, the place where Kira lived.

∾

The gardens were larger than he remembered; since his last visit almost two years before, she had expanded them, he saw. Thick clumps of yellow and deep pink flowers fringed the edge of the small dwelling with its hand-hewn beams and thatched roof. Matty had never paid attention to the names of flowers—boys generally disdained such things—

but now he wished he knew them, so that he could tell Jean.

Frolic went to the base of a wooden post that was entwined with a purple-blossomed vine, and lifted his leg to proclaim his presence and authority here.

The door to the cottage opened and Kira appeared there. She was wearing a blue dress and her long dark hair was tied back with a matching ribbon.

"Matty!" she cried in delight.

He grinned at her.

"And you've got yourself a new pup! I hoped you would. You were so sad, I remember, after Branchie died."

"His name is Frolic, and I'm afraid he's watering your . . ."

"Clematis. It's all right," she said, laughing. She reached for Matty and embraced him. Ordinarily uncomfortable with hugs, he would have stiffened his shoulders and drawn back; but now, from exhaustion and affection, he held Kira and to his own amazement felt his eyes fill with tears. He blinked them back.

"All right, stand back now and let me see you," she said. "Are you taller yet than I am?"

He stood back grinning and saw that they were eye to eye.

"Soon you will be. And your voice is almost a man's."

"I can read Shakespeare," he told her, swaggering.

"Hah! So can I!" she said, and he knew then for

certain how changed this village was, for in the earlier days, girls had not been allowed to learn.

"Oh, Matty, I remember when you were such a tiny thing, and so wild!"

"The Fiercest of the Fierce!" he reminded her, and she smiled fondly at him.

"You must be very tired. And hungry! You've just made such a long journey. Come inside. I have soup on the fire. And I want news of my father."

He followed her into the familiar cottage and waited while she reached for her walking stick that leaned against a wall and arranged it under her right arm. Dragging the useless leg, she took a thick earthen bowl from a shelf and went to the fire where a large pot simmered and smelled of herbs and vegetables.

Matty looked around. No wonder she had not wanted to leave this place. From the sturdy ceiling beams dangled the countless dried herbs and plants from which she made her dyes. Shelves on the wall were bright with rolls of yarn and thread arranged by color, white and palest yellow at one end, gradually deepening into blues and purples and then browns and grays at the other. On a threaded loom in the corner between two windows, a half-finished weaving pictured an intricate landscape of mountains, and he could see that she was now working on the sky and had woven in some feathery clouds of pink-tinged white.

She set the bowl of steaming soup on the table in

front of Matty and then went to the sink to pump water into a bowl for Frolic.

"Now. Tell me of Father," she asked. "He's well?"

"He's fine. He sends you his love."

He watched as Kira leaned her stick against the sink and knelt with difficulty to place the bowl on the floor. Then she called to Frolic, who was industriously chewing a broom in the corner.

When the puppy had come to her and turned his attention to the bowl of water, Kira rose again, sliced a thick piece from a loaf of bread, wedged her stick under her shoulder again, and brought the bread to the table. Matty watched the way she walked, the way she had always walked. Her right foot twisted inward, pulling the entire leg with it. The leg had not grown as the other had. It was shorter, turned, and useless.

He thanked her and dipped one end of the slice into his soup.

"He's a sweet puppy, Matty." He half listened as she chattered cheerfully about the dog. His thoughts had turned to Frolic's birth and how close to death the pup and his mother had been.

He glanced down at her twisted leg. How much more easily she would be able to walk—how much more steadily and quickly she would be able to travel—if the leg were straight, if the foot could be planted firmly on the ground.

He remembered the afternoon after the puppy and his mother had been saved. Today he was tired, very tired, from the long journey through Forest. But on that day, he had felt near death.

He tried to recall how long it had taken him to recover. He had slept, he knew. Yes. He remembered that he had slept for the afternoon, glad that the blind man had not been at home to ask why. But he had arisen before dinner—weary, still, but able to hide it, to eat and talk as if nothing had happened.

So his recovery had taken only a few hours, really. Still, it had been a puppy. Well, a puppy and its mother. *Two dogs.* He had fixed—cured? saved?—two dogs in late morning, and recovered from it by the end of the day.

"Matty? You're not listening! You're half asleep!" Kira's laughter was warm and sympathetic.

"I'm sorry." He put the last bit of bread into his mouth and looked apologetically at her.

"You're both tired. Look at Frolic."

He glanced over and saw the puppy sound asleep, curled into a mound of undyed yarn heaped near the door, as if the soft pile were a mother to doze against.

"I have work to do in the garden, Matty. The coreopsis needs staking and I've not had a chance to get to it. You lie down and get some rest, now, while I'm outside. Later we can talk. And you can go into the village and find your friends, for a visit."

He nodded and went to the couch to lie down on top of the knitted blanket that she had thrown across it. In his mind, he was counting the days they had left. He would explain to her that there was no time to visit with old pals.

He watched, his eyes heavy with exhaustion, as she took his bowl to the sink, placed it there, and then, leaning on her stick, gathered some stakes from a shelf, and a ball of twine. With her garden tools she turned to go outdoors. The twisted foot dragged in its familiar way. He had known everything about Kira for so long: her smile, her voice, her merry optimism, the amazing strength and skill of her hands, and the burden of her useless leg.

I must tell you this, Matty thought before he slept. *I can fix you.*

14

To his amazement, Kira said no. Not no to leaving—he hadn't suggested that to her, not yet—but a definite, unarguable no to the idea of a straightened, whole leg.

"This is who I am, Matty," she said. "It is who I have always been."

She looked at him fondly. But her voice was firm. It was evening. The fire glowed in the fireplace and she had lit the oil lamps. Matty wished that the blind man were in the room with them, playing his instrument, because the soft, intricate chords always brought a peace to their evenings together and he wanted Kira to hear the music, to feel the comfort it brought.

He had not yet told her that she was to return with him. During their supper together, as Kira chattered about the changes in the old village, how much better things were now, he had only half listened. In his mind he had been weighing what to tell her and when and how. There was so little time; and he needed, Matty knew, to present it to her in a decisive and convincing way.

But suddenly he heard her make a casual comment about her handicap. She was describing a small tapestry she had embroidered as a wedding gift for her friend Thomas, the woodcarver, who had recently been married.

"It was all finished and rolled up, and I decorated it with flowers," she said, "and on the morning of the wedding I set out, carrying it. But it had rained, and the path was wet, and I slipped and dropped the tapestry right into a mud puddle!" Kira laughed. "Luckily it was still early, so I came back here and was able to clean it. No one ever knew.

"My leg and stick are a nuisance when it's wet outdoors," she said. "My stick has never learned to navigate mud." She reached over to the pot and began to pour more tea into their mugs.

Surprising himself, he blurted it out. "I can fix your leg."

The room fell completely silent except for the hiss and crackle of the fire. Kira stared at Matty.

"I *can*," he said after a moment. "I have a gift. Your father says that you do, too, so you'll understand."

"I do," Kira agreed. "I always have. But my gift doesn't fix twisted things."

"I know. Your father told me yours is different."

Kira looked down at her hands, wrapped around her mug of tea. She opened her fingers, spread her hands upon the table, and turned them over. Matty could see the slender palms and the strong fingers, calloused at their tips from the garden work, the loom, and the needles that she used for her complicated, beautiful tapestries. "Mine is in my hands," she said softly. "It happens when I make things. My hands . . ."

He knew he shouldn't interrupt. But time was so short. So he cut her off, and apologized for it. "Kira, I want you to tell me all about your gift. But later. Right now there are important things to do and decide.

"I'm going to show you something," he told her. "Watch this. My gift is in my hands, too."

He had not planned this. But it seemed necessary. On the table lay the sharp knife with which she had sliced bread for their supper. Matty picked it up. He leaned down, and pulled the left leg of his trousers up. Kira watched, her eyes confused. Quickly, without flinching, he punctured his own knee. Dark red blood trickled in a thin crooked line down his lower leg.

"Oh!" Kira gasped. She stared at him and held her hand to her mouth. "What . . . ?"

Matty swallowed, took a deep breath, closed his eyes, and placed both of his hands on his wounded knee. He felt it coming. He felt his veins begin to pulsate; then the vibration coursed through him, and he felt the power leave his hands and enter his wound. It lasted no more than a few seconds and ended.

He blinked, and took his hands away. They were smeared slightly with blood. The trickled line on his leg had already begun to dry there.

"Matty! Whatever are you . . . ?" When he gestured, Kira leaned forward and looked carefully at his knee. After a moment she reached for the woven napkin on the table, dipped it into her tea, and wiped his leg with the damp cloth. The line of blood disappeared. His knee was smooth, unblemished. There was no wound at all. She looked intently at it, then bit her lip, reached out, and pulled the hem of his trouser leg down over his knee.

"I see." It was all she said.

Matty shook himself free of the wave of fatigue it had caused. "It was a very small wound," he explained. "I just did it to show you I could. It didn't take much out of me. But I've done it with bigger things, Kira. With other creatures. With much larger wounds."

"Humans?"

"Not yet. But I can do it. I can feel it, Kira. With a gift, you *know*."

She nodded. "Yes. That's true." She glanced at her own hands, resting there on the table, still holding the damp cloth.

"Kira, your leg will take a great deal out of me. I'll have to sleep, after, maybe for a whole day or even longer. And I don't have much time."

She looked at him quizzically. "Time for what?"

"I'll explain. But for now, I think we should start. If I do it right away, I can sleep completely through the night and almost all of the morning. You can use

121

that time to become accustomed to being whole . . ."

"I *am* whole," she said defiantly.

"I meant to having two strong legs. You'll be amazed at how it feels, at how much more easily you can move around. But it will take a little while to adjust to it."

She stared at him. She looked down at her twisted leg.

"Why don't you lie down over there on the couch? I'll pull this chair over and sit beside you." Matty began kneading his hands in preparation. He took several deep breaths and felt energized. He could tell that his full strength was back. The knee wound had been such a small thing, really.

He rose, lifted his wooden chair, and moved it over beside the couch where he had napped that afternoon. He arranged the cushions so that she would be comfortable. Behind him he heard Kira rise from her chair as well, lift her stick from where it leaned against the table, and walk across the room. To his surprise, when he turned, he saw that she had taken the mugs to the sink and was beginning to wash them, as if it were an ordinary evening.

"Kira?"

She looked over at him. She frowned slightly. Then she said no.

There was no arguing with her, none at all. After a while Matty gave up the attempt.

Finally he moved his chair again so that he could sit in front of the fire. It was chilly in the evenings now, with summer ending. Forest had been downright cold at night, and he had woken in the mornings during his journey aching and chilled. It was comforting to sit here by the warm fire now.

Kira picked up a small wooden frame with a half-finished piece of embroidery stretched taut across it. She brought it to her chair, and moved a basket filled with bright threads to the floor beside her. Then she leaned her stick against the fireplace wall, sat down, and picked up the needle that was waiting, threaded with green, attached to the fabric.

"I will go with you," she said quite suddenly in her soft voice. "But I will go as I am. With my leg. With my stick."

Matty, puzzled, stared at her. How had she known, before he asked it, what he was planning to ask of her?

"I was going to explain," he said after a long moment. "I was going to persuade you. How . . . ?"

"I started to tell you earlier," she said, "about my gift. What my hands do. Move your chair closer and I'll show you now."

He did so, pulling the crude wooden chair near to where she was. She tilted the embroidery frame so that he could see. Like the colorful tapestry on the wall of the blind man's house, this was a landscape. The stitches were tiny and complicated, and each section a subtle variation in color, so that deep green moved gradually into a slightly lighter shade, and then again lighter, until at the edges it was a pale yellow. The colors combined to form an exquisite pattern of trees, with the tiniest of individual leaves outlined in countless numbers.

"It's Forest," Matty said, recognizing it.

Kira nodded. "Look beyond it," she said, and extended her finger to point to a section in the upper right, where Forest opened and tiny houses were patterned around curved paths.

He thought he could almost make out the house he shared with the blind man, though it was infinitely small on the fabric.

"Village," he said, examining with awe the meticulousness of her craft.

"I embroider this scene again and again," Kira said, "and sometimes—not always—my hands begin to move in ways I don't understand. The threads seem to take on a power of their own."

He leaned closer to look more carefully at the embroidery. It was astounding, the detail of it, how tiny it was.

"Matty?" she said. "I've never done this with anyone watching. But I can feel it in my hands right now. Watch."

He peered intently as her right hand picked up the needle threaded with green. She inserted it into the fabric at an unfinished place near the edge of Forest. Suddenly both of her hands began to vibrate slightly. They *shimmered*. He had seen this once before, on the day that Leader stood at the window, gathered himself, and saw beyond.

He looked up at her face and saw that her eyes were closed. But her hands were moving very quickly now. They reached into the basket again and again, changed threads in a motion so fast he could barely follow it, and the needle entered the cloth, and entered the cloth, and entered the cloth.

Time seemed to stop. The fire continued to crackle and sputter. Frolic sighed in his sleep at the edge of the hearth. Matty sat speechless, watching the shimmering hands dart; hours and days and weeks seemed to go by, yet oddly, only a blink, an instant, of time passed. Today and tomorrow and yesterday were all spun together and held in those hands that moved and moved and moved, yet her eyes were closed, and the fire still flickered and the dog still slept.

Then it ended.

Kira opened her eyes, sat up straighter, and stretched her shoulders. "It tires me," she explained, though he already knew it.

"Look now," she said. "Quickly, because it will fade."

He leaned forward and saw that now, in the embroidered scene, at the bottom, two tiny people were entering Forest. He recognized one as himself, backpack on his back; he could even see, amazingly, the torn place on the sleeve of his jacket. Behind him, meticulously stitched in shades of brown, was Frolic, his tail high. And beside Frolic he saw Kira, her blue dress, her stick wedged under her arm, her dark hair tied back.

The top edge of the embroidery had changed as well. Now, beside the house he had recognized as his, he could see the blind man standing. His posture was that of someone waiting for something.

And suddenly Matty could see, too, crowds of people at the edge of Village. They were dragging huge logs. Someone—it looked like Mentor—was giving directions. They were preparing to build a wall.

Matty sat back. He blinked, astounded, then leaned forward to look at it again. He realized he wanted to search the scene for a glimpse of Jean. But now the details were gone. He could still see the colored stitches, but it was a simple—exquisitely beautiful, but simple—landscape again. For a moment he saw the people, flat now, with no detail, but then they faded abruptly and were gone.

Kira set the embroidery frame down on the floor and rose from her chair. "We must leave in the morning," she said. "I'll prepare food."

Matty was still stunned by what he had just seen. "I don't understand," he said.

"Do you understand what happened when you stabbed your knee with that knife and then closed and cured the wound with your hands?"

"No," he admitted. "I don't. It's my gift. That's all."

"Well," Kira said matter-of-factly, "this is mine. My hands create a picture of the future. Yesterday morning I held that same fabric and saw you come out of Forest. In the afternoon I opened the door and there you were."

She chuckled. "I hadn't seen Frolic, though. He was a nice surprise." The dog awoke and looked up at the sound of his name. He came to her to be patted.

"While you napped," she went on, "I stitched again and saw Father waiting for me. That was just this afternoon. Now they have started to move the logs into place for the wall. And—did you notice the change in Forest, Matty?"

He shook his head. "I was looking at the people."

"Forest is thickening. So we must hurry, Matty."

Odd. It was the same thing that Leader had seen. "Kira?" Matty asked.

"Yes?" She was taking food from a cupboard.

"Did you see a young man with blue eyes? About your age? We call him Leader."

She stood still for a moment, thinking. A strand of dark hair fell across her face, and she brushed it back with her hand. Then she shook her head. "No," she said. "But I *felt* him."

15

They woke early. The sun was just rising, and through the window Matty could see that the gardens were bathed in amber light. Thick around a tall trellis, a vine that had been simply green when he arrived the day before was now profuse with opened blue and white morning glories. Beyond the trellis, on tall stalks, tiny aster blossoms, deep pink with golden centers, trembled in the dawn breeze.

He felt her presence, suddenly, and turned to see Kira standing behind him, looking out.

"It will be hard for you to leave this," he said.

But she smiled and shook her head. "It's time. I always knew the time would come. I told my father that long ago."

"He says you'll have a garden there. He wanted me to tell you that."

She nodded. "Eat quickly, Matty, and we'll go. I've fed Frolic already."

∾

"Do you need help?" Matty asked, his mouth full of

the sweet muffin she had given him, as he watched her arrange a wrapped bundle on her back, criss-crossing the straps that held it around her chest. "What's in it?"

"No, I can do it just fine. It's my frame and some needles and thread."

"Kira, the journey's hard and long. There won't be time to sit and sew." Then Matty fell quiet. Of course she needed this. It was the way her gift came.

She had put food inside Matty's pack as well as in his rolled blanket. It was heavier than it had been coming, for there were two of them now. But Matty felt strong. He was almost relieved that she had not allowed him to mend her leg, for it would have weakened him badly, cost them perhaps several days as he rested from it, and sent them out less prepared and more vulnerable.

He could see, too, that she was accustomed to her stick and twisted leg. A lifetime of walking in that way had made it, as she had pointed out, part of her. It was who she was. To become a fast-striding Kira with two straight legs would have been to become a different person. This was not a journey Matty could undertake with a stranger.

"Frolic, if you were a little bigger and less frisky, I would strap a pack to your back," Kira said, laughing, to the eager puppy, who stood beside the door with his tail churning in the air. He could tell they were leaving. He was not going to be left behind.

Soon they were loaded with everything they had

packed so carefully the night before.

"We're ready, then," Kira announced, and Matty nodded in agreement. From the open doorway, with Frolic already outside sniffing the earth, they looked back to the large room that had been Kira's home since she had been a young girl. She was leaving the loom, the baskets of yarn and thread, the dried herbs on the rafters, the wall-hangings, the earthen mugs and plates made for her by the village potter, and a handsome wooden tray that had been a gift long ago from her friend Thomas, who had carved it with intertwined, complicated designs. From hooks along the wall hung her clothes, things she had made, some of them skirts and jackets rich with embroidered and appliquéd designs. Today she was wearing her simple blue dress and a heavy knitted sweater with buttons made from small flat stones.

She closed the door on all of it. "Come, Frolic," Matty called, unnecessarily. The dog scampered to them and raised his leg one last time against the doorsill, saying, in his way, "I have been here."

Then Matty moved toward the place where the path entered Forest. Kira, leaning on her stick, followed him, and Frolic, ears up, came behind.

∽

"You know," Kira said, "I've walked the forest path between this cottage and the center of my village so many times." Then she laughed. "Well, of course you know that, Matty. You did it with me when you were a little boy."

"I did. Again and again."

"But I have never once entered Forest. There was no need, of course. And it always seemed frightening somehow."

They had barely entered, and behind them the light of the clearing still showed, and a corner of Kira's little house. But ahead, Matty could see, the path was oddly dark. He didn't remember it being so dark.

"Are you frightened now?" he asked her.

"Oh, no, not with you. You know Forest so well."

"That's true. I do." It *was* true, but even as he said it, Matty felt a sense of discomfort, though he hid it from Kira. The path ahead did not seem to be as familiar as it had always been. He could tell that it was the same path—the turnings were the same; as he led her around the next one, the clearing behind them was no longer visible—but things that had seemed easy and accustomed no longer did. Now everything felt a little different: slightly darker, and decidedly hostile.

But he said nothing. He led the way, and Kira, strong despite her handicap, trudged after him.

◦∾◦

"They have entered."

Leader turned from the window. He had stood there for a long moment, intent, focused, while

131

beside him the blind man waited. They had been doing this for several days.

Leader sat to rest. He breathed hard. He was accustomed to this, the way his body temporarily lost its vigor and needed to restore itself after he had looked beyond.

The blind man gave a sigh that was clearly one of relief. "So she came with him."

Leader nodded, still not ready to talk.

"I worried that she wouldn't. It meant leaving so much behind. But Matty convinced her. Good for him."

Leader stretched, and sipped from the glass of water on his desk. Then he was able to speak. "She didn't need convincing. She could tell that it was time. She has that gift."

The blind man went to the window and stood there listening. Heavy dragging sounds and thuds were accompanied by shouts:

"Over here!"

"Put it down there!"

"Watch out!"

They could hear Mentor's voice, loud above the others. "Stack them right there," he directed. "Five to a stack. You! You idiot! Stop that! If you aren't going to help, go someplace else!"

Leader winced. "It was such a short time ago that he was so patient and soft-spoken. Listen to him now."

"Tell me how he looks," the blind man said.

Leader went to the window and looked down at the place where they were preparing to build the wall. He found Mentor in the crowd. "His bald spot is completely gone," he said. "He's taller. Or at least stands straighter. He's lost weight. And his chin is firmer than it was."

"A strange trade for him to have made," the blind man commented.

Leader shrugged. "For a woman," he pointed out. "People do strange things."

"I suppose it's too soon for you to look beyond again." The blind man was still at the window. His posture was uneasy.

Leader smiled. "You know it is. They've only just entered. They're fine."

"How much time do they have?"

"Ten days. The wall can't go up for ten days, according to the edict. It's enough time."

"Matty's like a son to me. It's as if both my children are out there."

"I know." Leader put a reassuring arm across the blind man's shoulders. "Come back here tomorrow morning and we'll look again."

"I'll go work in my garden. I'm preparing flower beds for Kira."

"Good idea. It'll take your mind from the worry."

But when Seer had gone, Leader stood at the window for a while, listening to the wall builders at their preparations. He was very worried himself. He had not told the blind man. But while he had watched Matty, Kira, and the puppy enter Forest, he had been able to see, too, that Forest was shifting, moving, thickening, and preparing to destroy them.

16

"I'll catch fish farther along," Matty said. "Frolic won't eat it, but you and I can. And there are berries and nuts. So we don't have to save this. Eat all you want."

Kira nodded and took a bite from the deep red apple he had given her. "It will be good to reduce the weight in your pack," she pointed out. "We can move more quickly then."

They were seated on the blanket in the place Matty had chosen to spend the first night. They had covered quite a distance during the day. He was surprised at how well she was able to keep up the pace.

"No, Frolic, not my stick." Kira scolded the little dog affectionately when he tried to use her cane as a plaything to chew. "Here," she said to him, and picked up a stick from the ground. She threw it to him and he dashed away with it, growling playfully, hoping that someone would chase him. When no one did, he lay down and attacked the stick like a warrior, tearing its bark with his small sharp teeth.

Matty tossed some dead twigs onto the fire he had built. It was close to dark now, and chilly. "We walked a long way today," he told Kira. "I'm amazed at how well you manage. I thought that because of your leg . . ."

"I'm so accustomed to it. I've always walked like this." Kira untied her leather sandals and began to rub her feet. "I'm tired, though. And look. I'm bleeding." She leaned forward with the hem of her skirt bunched in her hand, and wiped blood from the sole of her foot. "I'll throw this dress away when we arrive." She laughed. "Will there be fabric there so that I can make new clothes?"

Matty nodded. "Yes. There's plenty in the marketplace. And you can borrow clothes, too, from my friend Jean. She's about your size."

Kira looked at him. "Jean?" she said. "You've not mentioned her before."

He grinned and was glad it was dark so she wouldn't see his face turning crimson. It startled him that he had blushed. What was happening? He had known Jean for years. They had played together as children after his arrival in Village. He had tried, once, to tease and frighten her with a snake, only to discover that she loved garden snakes.

To Kira, now, he just shrugged. "She's my friend.

"She's pretty," he added, then cringed, embarrassed that he had said that, and waited for Kira to tease him. But she wasn't really listening. She was examining her feet, and he could see, even in the flickering light of the fire, that the soles were badly cut and bleeding.

She dipped the hem of her dress into the bowl of water they had set out for Frolic, and wiped the wounds. Watching her in the firelight, Matty could see her wince.

"How bad is it?" he asked.

"It will be all right. I've brought some herbal salve and I'll rub it in." He watched as she opened a pouch she took from her pocket and began to treat the punctures and cuts.

"Is there something wrong with your shoes?" he asked, glancing at the soft leather sandals set side by side on the ground. They had firm soles and she had seemed to walk comfortably in them.

"No. My shoes are fine. It's strange, though. While we were walking, I kept having to stop to pull twigs out of my shoes. You probably noticed." She laughed. "It was as if the underbrush was actually *reaching in* to poke at me."

She rubbed a little more ointment into the wounds on her feet. "It poked me *hard,* too. Maybe tomorrow I'll wrap some cloth around my feet before I put my sandals back on."

"Good idea." Matty didn't let her see how uneasy this made him feel. He fed the fire again and then arranged some rocks around it so that it couldn't escape from the little cleared space where he had built it. "We should sleep now, and get an early start tomorrow."

Soon, curled on the ground beside her, with Frolic between them and the blanket thrown across all three, Matty listened. He heard Kira's even breathing; she had fallen asleep immediately. He felt Frolic stir and turn in his light puppyish slumber, probably dreaming of birds and chipmunks to chase. He heard the last shifting of the sticks in the fire as it died and turned to ash. He heard the whoosh and flutter of an owl as it dived, and then the tiny squeal of a doomed rodent caught in its talons.

From the direction toward which they were traveling, he perceived a hint of the stench that permeated the deep center of Forest. By Matty's calculations, they would not reach the center for three days. He was surprised that already the foul smell of decay drifted to where they were resting. When finally he slept, his dreams were layered over with an awareness of rot and the imminence of terrible danger.

∾

In the morning, after they had eaten, Kira wrapped both of her feet in fabric torn from her petticoat, and when the wrappings were thick and protective, she loosened the straps of her sandals and fit her bandaged feet carefully into them.

Then she picked up her stick and walked a bit around the fire to test the arrangement. "Good," she said after a moment. "It's quite comfortable. I won't have a problem."

Matty, rolling the blanket around the remains of their food, glanced over. "Tell me if it happens again, the sticks and twigs poking at you."

She nodded. "Ready, Frolic?" she called, and the puppy scampered to her from the bushes where he had been pawing at a rodent's hole. Kira adjusted her wrapped bundle of embroidery tools on her back and prepared to follow Matty as he set off.

To his surprise, he had some difficulty finding the path this second morning. That had never happened before. Kira waited patiently behind him as he investigated several apparent entrances from the clearing where they had slept.

"I've come through here so often," he told her, puzzled. "I've slept in this same place so many times before. And I've always kept the path clear and easy to find. But now . . ."

He pushed back some bushes with his hand, stared for a moment at the ground he had revealed, then took his knife from his pocket and pruned back the branches. "Here," he said, pointing. "Here's the path. But the bushes have somehow grown across and hidden it. Isn't that strange? I just came through here a day and a half ago. I'm sure it wasn't overgrown like this then."

He held the thick shrubbery back to make it easier for Kira to enter, and was pleased to see that her footsteps, despite her injured feet, seemed firm and without pain.

"I can push things with my stick," she told him. "See?" She raised her stick and used it to force up a thick vine that had reached from one tree to another on the other side of the path, making a barrier at the height of their shoulders. Together they ducked and went under the vine. But immediately they could see that there were others ahead, barring their approach.

"I'll cut them," Matty said. "Wait here."

Kira stood waiting, Frolic suddenly quiet and wary at her feet, while Matty sliced through the vines at eye level ahead of them.

"Ow," he said, and winced. An acidic sap dripped from the cut vines and burned where it landed on his arm. It seemed to eat through the thin cotton fabric of his sleeve. "Be careful not to let it drip on you," he called to Kira, and motioned to her to come forward.

They made their way carefully through the passageway, which was a maze of vines, Matty in front with his knife. Again and again the sap spattered onto his arms until his sleeves were dotted with holes and the flesh beneath was burned raw. Their progress was very slow, and when finally the path widened, opened, and was free of the glistening growth—which they could see had already, amazingly, regrown and reblocked the path they had just walked—they stopped to rest. It had begun to rain. The trees were so thick above them that the downpour barely penetrated, but the foliage dripped and was cold on their shoulders.

"Do you have more of that herbal salve?" Matty asked.

Kira took it from her pocket and handed it to him. He had pushed back his sleeves and was examining his arms. Inflamed welts and oozing blisters had made a pattern on his skin.

"It's from the sap," he told her, and rubbed the salve onto the lesions.

"I guess my sweater was thick enough to protect me. Does it hurt?"

"No, not much." But it wasn't true. Matty didn't want to alarm her, but he was in excruciating pain, as if his arms had been burned by fire. He had to hold his breath and bite his tongue to keep from crying out as he applied the salve.

For a brief moment, he thought that he might try to use his gift, to call forth the vibrating power and eradicate the stinging poisonous rash on his arms. But he knew he must not. It would take too much out of him—it would, in Leader's words, *spend his gift*—and it would hamper their progress. They had to keep moving. Something so terrifying was happening that Matty did not even try to assess it.

Kira did not know. She had never made this journey before. She could feel the difficulties of this second day but did not realize they were unusual. She found herself able to laugh, not aware of the incredible pain that Matty was feeling in his singed and blistered arms. "Goodness," she said, chuckling, "I'm glad my clematis doesn't grow that fast or that thick. I'd never be able to open my front door."

Matty rolled his sleeves back down over the painful burns and returned the salve to Kira. He forced himself to smile.

Frolic was whimpering and trembling. "Poor thing," Kira said, and picked him up. "Was that path scary? Did some of the sap drip on you?" She handed him to Matty.

He saw no wounds on the puppy, but Frolic was unwilling to walk. Matty tucked him inside his jacket, curling the ungainly legs and feet, and the puppy nestled there against his chest. He felt the little heart beat against his own.

"What's that smell?" Kira asked, making a face. "It's like compost."

"There's a lot of decaying stuff in the center of Forest," he told her.

"Does it get worse?"

"I'm afraid it will."

"How do you get through it? Do you tie a cloth around your nose and mouth?"

He wanted to tell her the truth. *I've never smelled it before. I've come through here a dozen, maybe two dozen, times, but I have never smelled it before. The vines have never been there. It has never been like this before.*

Instead, he said, "That's the best method, I suppose. And your salve has a nice herbal odor. We'll rub some of it on our upper lips, so it will block that foul smell."

"And we'll hurry through," she suggested.

"Yes. We'll go through as quickly as we can."

The searing sensation in his arms had subsided, and now they simply throbbed and ached.

142

But his body felt hot and weak, as if he were ill. Matty wanted to suggest that they stop here and rest, that they spread the blanket and lie down for a while. But he had never rested at midday on previous journeys. And now they could not afford the time. They had to move forward, toward the stench. At least the vines were behind them now, and he didn't see any ahead.

The cold rain continued to fall. He remembered, suddenly, how Jean's hair curled and framed her face when it was damp. In contrast to the horrible stench that was growing stronger by the minute, he remembered the fragrance of her when she had kissed him goodbye. It seemed so long ago.

"Come," he said, and gestured to Kira to follow.

Leader told the blind man that Matty and Kira had made it through the first night and were well into the second day. He murmured it from the chair where he was resting, lacking the strength to talk in his usual firm voice.

"Good," the blind man said cheerfully, unsuspecting. "And the puppy? How's Frolic? Could you see him?"

Leader nodded. "He's fine."

The truth was that the puppy was in better condition than Matty himself, Leader knew. So was Kira. Leader could see that Kira had had problems the first day, when Forest had punctured and wounded her. His gift had given him a glimpse of her bleeding feet. He had watched her rub on the salve and wince, and he had winced in sympathy. But she was managing well now. He could see, but did not tell the blind man, that now Forest was attacking Matty instead.

And he could see as well that they had not yet approached the worst of it.

17

By the second afternoon Matty was in agony, and he knew there was still a day to go before the worst of it. His arms, poisoned by the sap, had festered and were seeping, swollen, and hot. The path was almost entirely overgrown now, and the bushes clawed at him, scraping at the infected burns until he was close to sobbing with the pain.

He could no longer delude Kira into thinking this was an ordinary journey. He told her the truth.

"What should we do?" she asked him.

"I don't know," he said. "We could try to go back, I suppose, but you can see that the path back is blocked already. I don't think we could find the way, and I know I can't go through those vines again. Look at my arms."

He gingerly pulled back his ruined sleeve, and showed her. Kira gasped. His arms no longer looked like human limbs. They had swollen until the skin itself had split and was oozing a yellowish fluid.

"We're close to the center now," he explained, "and once we get through that, we'll be on the way out. But we still have a long way to go, and it will most likely get a lot worse than it is already."

She followed him, uncomplaining, for there was no other choice, but she was pale and frightened.

When they came, finally, to the pond where he ordinarily refilled his water container and sometimes caught some fish, he found it stagnant. Once clear and cool, the water was now dark brown, clogged with dead insects, and it smelled of kinds of filth he could only guess at.

So they were thirsty now.

The rain had stopped, but it left them clammy and cold.

The smell was much, much worse.

Kira smoothed the herbal salve on their upper lips and wrapped cloth around their noses and mouths to filter the stench. Frolic huddled, head down, inside Matty's shirt.

Suddenly the path, the same path he had always followed, ended abruptly at a swamp that had never been there before. Sharp, knifelike reeds grew from glistening mud. There was no way around. Matty stared at it and tried to make a plan.

"I'm going to cut a thick piece of vine, Kira, to use as rope. Then I'll tie us together, so that if one of us should get stuck in some way . . ."

Bending his grotesquely swollen arm with difficulty, he reached with his knife and severed a length of heavy vine.

"I'll tie it," Kira said. "I'm good at that. I've knotted so much yarn and thread." Deftly she circled his waist, and then her own, with the length of supple vine. "Look," she told him, "it's quite fast." She tugged at the knots, and he could see that she had done a masterly job of connecting them to each other, leaving a length of vine between.

"I'll go first," Matty said, "to test the mud. The thing I'm most concerned about . . ."

Kira nodded. "I know. There are muds called quicksand."

"Yes. If I start to sink, you must pull hard to help me get out. I'll do the same for you."

Inch by inch they moved through the swamp, looking for thickets of growth on which to place their feet, testing the suction when they were forced into the thick mud. The razor-sharp reeds sliced mercilessly into their legs and mosquitoes feasted on the fresh blood. From time to time they pulled each other free when they were caught by the suction. Kira's sandals, first one and then the other, were sucked from her feet and disappeared.

Miraculously, Matty's shoes remained, coated with the slippery mud so that he appeared to be wearing heavy wet boots by the time he dragged himself from the other side of the swamp. He waited there, holding the vine rope steady, easing Kira through the mud and up the bank.

Then he used the knife and cut through the vine that had held them together in the swamp. "Look!" he said, pointing to his feet, encased in mud that was already drying into a crust. For a moment he had an odd desire to laugh at the grotesque thick boots.

Then he saw Kira's bare feet and shuddered. They were raw, dripping with blood from the reopened cuts she had previously suffered, and from new lacerations caused by the sharp swamp reeds. Matty climbed back down the bank, scooped wet mud with his hands, and gently coated her feet and legs, stopping the bleeding and trying to ease her pain with the thick cool paste.

He looked up through the tree growth to the sky, trying to assess the time of day. It had taken them a long time to cross the swamp. His arms were unusable, but he could still hold the knife in his swollen hands. Kira, her legs and feet in muddied shreds, knelt beside him, trying to catch her breath. The stench made it difficult for them to breathe, and he could feel the puppy choking from it inside his shirt.

He forced himself to speak with optimism.

"Follow me," he said. "I think the center is just ahead. And night is coming soon. We'll find a place to sleep, and then in the morning we'll start the final bit. Your father's waiting."

Slowly he moved forward, and Kira rose onto her ruined feet and followed him.

❧

Matty felt his reason leave him now and again, and he began to imagine that he was outside of his own body. He liked that, escaping the pain. In his mind he drifted overhead, looking down on a struggling boy who pushed relentlessly through the dark, thorny undergrowth, leading a crippled girl. He felt sorry for the pair and wanted to invite them to soar and hover comfortably with him. But his bodiless self had no voice, and he was unable to call down to where they were.

These were daydreams, escapes, and they didn't last long.

"Can we stop for a minute? I need to rest. I'm sorry." Kira's voice was weak, and muffled by the cloth covering her mouth.

"Up here. There's a little opening. We'll have room to sit down." Matty pointed, and pushed ahead to the place he had seen. When they reached it, he shook his rolled blanket from his back and set it on the ground as a cushion. They sank down beside each other.

"Look." Kira pointed to the skirt of her dress, to show him. The blue fabric, discolored now, was in shreds. "The branches seem to reach for me," she said. "They're like knives. They cut my clothes" — she examined the ruined dress, with its long ragged tears — "but they don't quite reach my flesh. It's as if they're waiting. Teasing me."

For a terrible instant Matty remembered how Ramon had described poor Stocktender, who had been entangled by Forest and whose body had been found strangled by vines. He wondered if Forest had teased Stocktender first, burning and cutting him before the final moments of his hideous death.

"Matty? Say something."

He shook himself. He had let his mind drift again. "I'm sorry," he said. "I don't know what to say.

"How are your feet?" he thought to ask her.

He saw her shudder, and looked down. The encrusted mud he had applied as balm had fallen away. Her feet were nothing more than ragged flesh.

"And look at your poor arms," she said. His torn sleeves were stained with seepage from his wounds.

He remembered the days of Village in the past, when a person who had difficulty walking would be helped cheerfully by someone stronger. When a person with an injured arm would be tended and assisted till he healed.

He heard sounds all around them and thought them to be the sounds of Village: soft laughter, quiet conversation, and the bustle of daily work and happy lives. But that was an illusion born of memory and yearning. The sounds he heard were the rasping croak of a toad, the stealthy movement of a rodent in the bushes, and foamy bubbles belching from some slithery malevolent creature in the dark waters of the pond.

"I'm really having trouble breathing," Kira said.

Matty realized that he was, too. It was the heaviness of the air with its terrible smell. It was like a foul pillow held tightly to their faces, cutting off their air, choking them. He coughed.

He thought of his gift. Useless now. Probably he

still had the strength and power to repair his own wounded arms or Kira's tortured feet. But then the next onslaught would come, and the next, and he would be too weakened to resist it. Even now, looking listlessly down, he saw a pale green tendril emerge from the lower portion of a thorny bush and slide silently toward them. He watched in a kind of fascination. It moved like a young viper: purposeful, silent, and lethal.

Matty took his knife from his pocket again. When the sinister, curling stem—in appearance not unlike the pea vines that grew in early summer in their garden—reached his ankle, it began to curl tightly around his flesh. Quickly he reached down and severed it with the small blade. Within seconds it turned brown and fell away from him, lifeless.

But there seemed no victory to it. Only a pause in a battle he was bound to lose.

He noticed Kira reaching for her pack and spoke sharply to her. "What are you doing? We have to move on a minute. It's dangerous here." She hadn't seen the deadly thing that had grabbed at Matty, but he knew there would be more; he watched the bushes for them.

It had come for him first, he realized. He did not want to be the first to die, to leave her alone.

To his dismay, she was removing her embroidery tools. "Kira! There's no time!"

"I might be able to . . ." Then she deftly threaded a needle.

To what? he wondered bitterly. *To create a hand-some wall-hanging depicting our last hours?* He remembered that in the art books he had leafed through at Leader's, many paintings depicted death. A severed head on a platter. A battle, and the ground strewn with bodies. Swords and spears and fire; and nails being pounded into the tender flesh of a man's hands. Painters had preserved such pain through beauty.

Perhaps she would.

He watched her hands. They flew over the small frame, moving in and out with the needle. Her eyes were closed. She was not directing her own fingers. They simply moved.

He waited, his eyes vigilant, watching the surrounding bushes for the next attack. He feared the coming dark. He wanted to move on, out of this place, before evening came. But he waited while her hands moved.

Finally she looked up. "Someone is coming to help us," she said. "It's the young man with the blue eyes."

Leader.

"Leader's coming?"

"He has entered Forest."

Matty sighed. "It's too late, Kira. He'll never find us in time."

"He knows just where we are."

"He can see beyond," he said, and coughed. "Have I already told you that? I can't remember."

"See beyond?" She had begun to pack her things away.

"It's his gift. You see ahead. He sees beyond. And I . . ." Matty fell silent. He raised one hideously swollen arm and looked listlessly at the pus that seeped through the fabric of his sleeve. Then he laughed harshly. "I can fix a frog."

18

The blind man was alone now, with his fear, since Leader had gone. He had returned to his own house to wait, passing as he did the workers still preparing to build a wall surrounding Village.

In the yard beside the small homeplace he had shared happily with Matty for so long, he could smell the newly turned earth. Yesterday he had begun to dig a flower garden for his daughter, pushing in the spade and loosening the weeds for pulling.

Jean had stopped by to ask about Matty. She had admired Seer's work and told him she would bring seeds from her own flowers. They could have twin gardens, she said. She was looking forward to meeting the blind man's daughter. She had never had a big sister, and perhaps Kira would be that for her. He could hear the smile in her voice.

But that had been yesterday, and he had told Jean then, believing it to be true, that the travelers were fine, and on their way home.

This morning Leader, after standing motionless at the window for a long time, had told him the truth.

The blind man had cried out in anguish. "Both of

them? *Both of my children?*"

Ordinarily Leader needed to rest after he looked beyond. But now he did not take the time. The blind man could hear him moving about the room, gathering things.

"Don't let Village know I'm gone," Leader told him.

"Gone? Where are you going?" The blind man was still reeling with the news of what was happening in Forest.

"To save them, of course. But I don't trust the wall builders. If they realize I'm not here to remind everyone of the proclamation, I think they'll start early. I don't want to get back here and not be able to reenter."

"Can you slip past them?"

"Yes, I know a back way. And they're all so absorbed in their work that they won't be looking for me. I'm the last person they want to see, anyway. They know how I feel about the wall."

The blind man was encouraged out of his despair by the optimism in Leader's voice. *To save them, of course.* He had said that. Maybe it could be true.

"Do you have food? A warm jacket? Weapons? Maybe you'll need weapons. I hate the thought of it."

But Leader said no. "Our gifts are our weaponry," he said. Then he hurried down the stairs.

Now, alone in his homeplace, a feeling of hopelessness returned to the blind man. He reached for the wall beside the kitchen and felt the edges of the tapestry hanging there, the one Kira had made for him. He let his fingers creep across it, feeling their way through the embroidered landscape. He had felt the tiny, even stitches often before, because he went to it and touched it when he was missing her. Now, on this shattered morning, he felt nothing but knots and snarls under his fingertips. He felt death, and smelled its terrible smell.

19

Night was ending and they were still alive. Matty woke at dawn to find himself still curled next to Kira in the place where they had collapsed together after struggling as far as they could into the evening.

"Kira?" His voice was hoarse from thirst, but she heard him and stirred. She opened her eyes.

"I can't see very well," she whispered. "Everything is blurred."

"Can you sit up?" he asked.

She tried, and groaned. "I'm so weak," she said. "Wait." She took a deep breath and then painfully pushed herself into a sitting position.

"What's that on your face?" she asked him. He touched his upper lip where she pointed, and brought his hand away smeared with bright blood. "My nose is bleeding," he said, puzzled.

She handed him the cloth she had worn around her face the day before, and he held it against his nose to try to stem the flow of blood. "Do you think you can walk?" he asked her after a moment.

But she shook her head. "I'm sorry. I'm so sorry, Matty."

157

He wasn't surprised. After the thorny branches had shredded her dress, they had reached for her legs as night fell, and now he could see that she was terribly lacerated. The wounds were deep, and he could see exposed muscles and tendons glisten yellow and pink in a devastating kind of beauty where the ragged flesh gaped open.

Matty himself could probably still stumble along. But his arms were completely useless now, and his hands seemed no more than huge paws. He could no longer even hold the knife with any strength.

As for Frolic, he didn't know. The little dog lay motionless against his chest.

He watched dully as a brown lizard with a darting tongue scrambled across their blanket with its tail flicking.

"You go on," Kira murmured. She lay back down and closed her eyes. "I'll just sleep."

He moved his damaged arms with some difficulty to her pack, which lay beside her where she had dropped it the night before. Through a haze of pain he realized that his fingers still moved awkwardly at his will, and he used them to open her pack and remove the embroidery frame. Painstakingly, slowly, he threaded her needle. Then he shook her awake.

"Don't. I don't want to wake up."

"Kira," he said to her, "take this." He handed her the frame. "Just try one more time. Please. See where Leader is, if you can."

She blinked and looked at the frame as if it were

unfamiliar. Matty put the threaded needle into her right hand. He was remembering something. It was something he had said once, to Leader, about meeting halfway.

But she had closed her eyes again. He spoke loudly to her. "Kira! Put the needle into the fabric. And try to *meet* him. Try, Kira!"

Kira sighed, and with a feeble gesture she inserted the needle into the cloth as he held the frame for her. He watched her hands. Nothing happened. Nothing changed. *"Again,"* he implored.

He saw her hands flutter, and the shimmer came.

❧

Leader felt Forest's attack begin when he was two days in. Probably it had started earlier, with sharp twigs—he remembered now that one had barely missed his eye—but he had been so intent, then, on finding and following the path that he had not paid attention to the little wounds inflicted on him. He had strode through the deep woods with no thought of danger; he concentrated only on finding the pair that he had seen so close to death. He didn't eat or sleep.

He had begun to perceive the stench on the morning of the second day, and it served to hurry his steps. Without flinching, he brushed aside the grasping branches and ignored the thorns that scraped his arms and face.

He encountered a place where the path seemed simply to end. He stopped, puzzled, and examined the undergrowth. From somewhere nearby a shiny green frog emerged from the base of a bush.

Churrump.

Churrump.

It hopped and skittered toward him in the mud, then turned itself around and went forward. To his surprise, Leader followed the frog, pushing his way through thick bushes, and found that it had led him to the place where the path resumed. Relieved, for he had thought briefly that he was lost, he continued on. But now he recognized the attacks. Now he saw that it was not random thorny branches and his own clumsiness in walking into them, but rather an assault from Forest itself.

Suddenly the air surrounding him was abuzz with stinging insects. They flew at his face and bit mercilessly. He remembered, from his reading, descriptions of besieged medieval castles, and armies of men with bows sending so many arrows that the sky seemed thick with them. This felt like that. He felt pierced in a thousand places, and he cried out.

Then, just as suddenly, they were gone: regrouping, he thought, for another attack. He rushed forward, thinking to move away from this swampy area which harbored and bred such creatures. Indeed, the path did turn and led to drier ground, but here a sharp rock flung itself up and split the skin on his knee; then another sliced his hand so badly that he had to wrap the cut tightly in cloth for fear the loss of blood would weaken him beyond repair.

Stumbling and bleeding, he wished briefly that he had brought some kind of weapon. But what would have protected him against Forest itself? It was a force too huge to fight with a knife or a club.

Our gifts are our weaponry, he remembered saying to the blind man. It seemed so long ago that he had said it. He had felt certain of it at the time, but now he could not even think what he had meant.

He stood silently for a moment. His face was disfigured now, swollen from bites that oozed a dark fluid. Blood ran from his left ear, which had been gashed by a razor-sharp stone. One of his ankles was entangled by a vine that grew so quickly he could see it move, snaking its way toward his knee; he knew he would soon be immobilized by it, and the insects would return, then, to finish him off.

He faced what he knew to be the center of Forest, the place where Matty and Kira were trapped, and he willed himself to look beyond. It seemed the only thing left to do.

20

"What are you seeing?" Matty asked her in a hoarse voice.

But she didn't reply at first. Her eyes were closed. Her fingers moved as if in a dream. The needle went in and out, in and out.

He lifted his head to try to see. But his eyes were swollen, and when he raised himself, blood still flowed from his nose. So he lay back down, groaning from the effort, and in doing so felt the limp body of the puppy shift inside his shirt.

Matty had never experienced such an enormous sadness. His other dog had died in old age, peaceful and ready. But Frolic was only a puppy, new to life, and had been such a spirited creature, so curious and playful. It seemed impossible that he would have become a lifeless thing in such a short time.

But it was true of everything, he thought. His sadness was for all of it: for Village, no longer the happy place it had been; for Kira, no longer the sturdy, eager young woman he had always known. And Leader? He wondered what was happening to Leader now.

Suddenly Kira seemed to come awake. She whispered, "He's coming. He's close." Her voice was right beside him, very near to Matty's ear as he lay curled next to her. But it sounded, at the same time, far away, as if she were moving someplace distant.

✌

The vine around his ankle tugged at him, bit into his flesh, anchored itself there, and sent a new shoot upward. Another snaked itself out of the bushes and curled around his foot. Leader didn't notice. He stood immobile, alert. His eyes were open but he was no longer seeing the vermin-ridden trees around him, their blighted leaves, or the foul dark mud under his feet. He was looking beyond, and he was seeing something beautiful.

"Kira," he said, though it was his mind that spoke, for his human voice was inaudible now and his mouth was painfully swollen with open sores.

"We need you," she replied, and it was her mind speaking, too. Matty, beside her, heard nothing but the soft flutter of her fingers moving on the fabric.

✌

In the place called Beyond, Leader's consciousness met Kira's, and they curled around each other like wisps of smoke, in greeting.

"We are wounded," she told him, "and lost."

"I am hurt, too, and captured here," he replied.

With the exchange, they drifted dangerously apart. Where he stood, Leader could feel the vine now. His knee buckled as the sharp-toothed stem bit. He tried to reach for it but his hands were entangled, too.

With great effort, his consciousness touched hers again. "Ask the boy for help," he told her.

"Do you mean Matty?"

"Yes, though it is not his true name. Tell him we need his gift now. Our world does."

Matty felt Kira stir beside him. She opened her eyes. He watched as her tongue moved to moisten her blistered lips. When she spoke, her voice was so weak that he could not make out the words.

With difficulty he leaned painfully toward her, so that his ear was near her mouth.

"We need your gift," she whispered.

Matty fell back in despair. He had followed Leader's instructions. He had not spent the gift. He had not made Ramon well, had not fixed Kira's crooked leg, or even tried to save his little dog. But it was too late now. His body was so damaged he could barely move. He could no longer bend his ravaged arms. How could he place his hands on anything? And what, in any case, did she want him to touch? So much was ruined.

In agony and hopelessness, he turned away from her and rolled off the blanket and into the thick foul-smelling mud. With his arms outstretched, his hands touching the earth, he lay there waiting to die.

He felt his fingers begin to vibrate.

21

It began with the tiniest sensation. It was different from the larger feelings that still racked his body: the searing agony in his arms and hands, the almost unendurable ulceration of his parched mouth, the feverish pounding of his head.

This was a whispered hint of power. He felt it in the tips of his fingers, in the whorls and crevices of his outer skin. It moved across his hands as they lay motionless in the mud.

Though he shivered from illness and anguish, he could sense his blood beginning to warm and flow. He lay still. Inside him the thick dark liquid slid sinuously through his veins. It entered his heart and throbbed there, moving with purpose through the labyrinth of muscle, collecting energy that came faintly to it from his collapsing lungs. He could feel it surge into his arteries. Within the blood itself he could perceive its separate cells, and see their colors in his consciousness, and the prisms of their molecules, and all of it was awake now, gathering power.

He could feel his own nerves, each one, millions of them, taut with energy waiting to be released. The fibers of his muscles tightened.

Gasping, Matty called for his gift to come. There was no sense of how to direct it. He simply clawed at the earth, feeling the power in his hands enter, pulsating, into the ruined world. He became aware, suddenly, that he had been chosen for this.

Near him, Kira began to breathe more easily. What had been close to coma turned now to sleep.

Not far away, Leader tentatively lifted one foot and found it free of the entangling vine. He opened his eyes.

Back in Village, a breeze came up. It came through the windows of the homeplace where Ramon lived with his family. Ramon sat up suddenly in the bed, where he had lain ill for days, and felt the fever begin to seep from him.

The blind man sensed the breeze entering the open windows and lifting an edge of the tapestry on the wall. He felt the fabric, and found the stitches as even and smooth as they had been in the past.

Matty groaned and pressed his hands harder into the ground. All of his strength and blood and breath were entering the earth now. His brain and spirit became part of the earth. He rose. He floated above, weightless, watching his human self labor and writhe. He gave himself to it willingly, traded himself for all that he loved and valued, and felt free.

∽

Leader walked forward. He wiped his face with his hands and felt the lesions fade, as if they had been cleansed away. He could see the path clearly now, for the bushes had drawn back, their leaves bright with new green growth and dappled with buds. A yellow butterfly lit on a bush, paused, and darted off. Rounded stones bordered the path, and sunlight filtered down through the canopy of trees. The air was fresh, and he could hear a stream flowing nearby.

❧

Matty could see and hear everything. He saw Jean, beside her garden, call out in happy greeting to her father; and he saw Mentor, stooped once more, and balding, wave to her from the path where he was walking toward the schoolhouse with a book in his hand. His face was stained again with the birthmark, and poetry had returned to him. Matty heard him recite:

> Today, the road all runners come,
> Shoulder-high we bring you home,
> And set you at your threshold down,
> Townsman of a stiller town.

He saw the wall builders walk away from their work.

He heard the new ones singing in their own

languages—a hundred different tongues, but they understood one another. He saw the scarred woman standing proudly in their midst beside her son, and the people of Village gathered to listen.

He saw Forest and understood what Seer had meant. It was an illusion. It was a tangled knot of fears and deceits and dark struggles for power that had disguised itself and almost destroyed everything. Now it was unfolding, like a flower coming into bloom, radiant with possibility.

Drifting there, he looked down and saw his own self becoming motionless. He felt his breathing slow. He sighed, let go, and felt a sense of peace.

He watched Kira wake, and he saw Leader find her there.

∾

Kira took a cloth to the stream and brought it back, moistened, to wash Matty's still face. Leader had turned him over. She sobbed at the sight of him but was glad that his terrible wounds were gone. She bathed his arms and hands. The skin was firm and unblemished, without scars.

"I knew him when he was a little boy," she said, weeping. "He always had a dirty face and a mischievous spirit."

She smoothed his hair. "He called himself the Fiercest of the Fierce."

Leader smiled. "He was that. But it was not his true name."

Kira wiped her eyes. "He so hoped to receive his true name at the end of this journey."

"He would have."

"He wanted to be *Messenger*," Kira confided.

Leader shook his head. "No. There have been other messengers, and there will be more to come." He leaned down and placed his hand solemnly on Matty's forehead above the closed eyes. "Your true name is *Healer*," he said.

A sudden rustling in the bushes startled them both. "What's that?" Kira asked in alarm. At her voice, the puppy, his fur matted with twigs, emerged from the place where he had been hiding.

"It's Frolic!" Kira took him into her arms and he licked her hand.

Beside her, tenderly, Leader picked up what remained of the boy and prepared to carry him home. In the distance, the sound of keening began.

sweet dreams!

Littlest One is learning the art of giving dreams to humans. Each night she softly touches their beloved objects, gathers happy memories, and then presents these pleasant thoughts as dreams. But when her human is threatened by dark creatures, can Littlest One's gossamer touch protect him?